AS THE MOUNTED INDIAN RACED TOWARD HIM WITH A LANCE . . .

Nate instinctively raised the Hawken and went to fire, but in a flash of insight he realized the sound of the shot would carry to the Blackfeet and might lead them to his location. Instead of squeezing the trigger he darted to the right and dived for the ground. In his ears drummed the pounding hooves of the warrior's mount, and a second later something brushed his right shoulder and thudded into the earth at his side.

A tremendous whoop issued from bloodthirsty lips as the Indian bore down on him.

Rolling to the left, Nate tried to push erect. A heavy body slammed onto his back, stunning him, driving him down again, and he lost his grip on the rifle. Knees gouged him in the spine and strong hands looped around his chin from behind. He dimly comprehended the man was trying to break his neck . . . .

The *Wilderness* series
published by Leisure Books:

#1: *KING OF THE MOUNTAIN*
#2: *LURE OF THE WILD*
#3: *SAVAGE RENDEZVOUS*
#4: *BLOOD FURY*

WILDERNESS

Tomahawk Revenge

David Thompson

LEISURE BOOKS NEW YORK CITY

Dedicated to . . .
Judy, Joshua, and Shane

A LEISURE BOOK®

May 1991

Published by

Dorchester Publishing Co., Inc.
276 Fifth Avenue
New York, NY 10001

Printed in the United States of America.

Chapter One

The sharp retort carried for miles.

Those eagles and hawks soaring high above the nearby massive mountains heard it, as did the elk, deer, and buffaloes inhabiting the sea of verdant forest covering the slopes and valleys in all directions. Chipmunks ceased scampering, squirrels stopped chattering, and even bears paused to listen intently. All the song birds within hearing range fell silent. So alien a sound could only mean one thing. The most dangerous predator of all was abroad: man.

Borne by the stiff breeze, the sound echoed and reverberated, diminishing with the distance traveled, until finally another pair of ears heard it.

Up went a square chin as the listener cocked his head to one side. His broad shoulders straightened under his buckskins and his green eyes crinkled in concentration. A mane of black hair framed his rugged features. Tied at the back, suspended with the quill jutting upward, was an eagle feather. A powder horn and a bullet pouch were slanted across his muscular chest. Wedged under his brown leather belt were two flintlock pistols, one on either side of the buckle. A butcher knife in a beaded sheath dangled from his left hip. Held in his left hand was a Hawken rifle obtained months before in St. Louis.

The brawny nineteen-year-old lowered his head when the sound died away and beat a hasty path to the northeast, crossing a low ridge and descending to a wide stream meandering through a scenic valley. He turned upstream and scoured both banks until he spied another figure ahead. "Shakespeare!"

The object of the young man's attention glanced around. He also wore fringed buckskins, while on his head rested a brown beaver hat that scarcely contained his bushy gray hair. A beard and mustache of the same color gave his weathered face a grizzled aspect. Eyes the hue of a clear alpine lake regarded the younger man expectantly. A bullet pouch and powder horn adorned his person, as did a single flintlock and a butcher knife. Held in the crook of his right arm was a rifle.

"Did you hear that shot?" asked the youthful mountaineer as he approached.

"I might be getting on in years, but my ears still work just fine," responded Shakespeare. "Is that what has you so excited?"

"It could be Indians."

"It could, Nate," Shakespeare admitted. "It could also be another trapper hunting game for his supper, like you're supposed to be doing."

"I saw an elk and was following its tracks when I heard the shot and figured I'd better get back to you."

"Afraid I can't handle myself?"

"Of course not. There isn't a white man alive who knows these Rocky Mountains better than you do. But we are in Ute country, and we both know they hate all trappers. If they cut our trail they'll go out of their way to hunt us down and kill us."

"Whoever did the shooting is miles from here. Even if it is a band of Utes, I doubt we have anything to worry about."

Nathaniel King gazed to the west at a snow-crowned peak and hoped his mentor was right. The last thing he wanted was another run-in with hostile Indians. Since venturing into the Great American Desert, as the land west of the Mississippi River was known back in the States, he'd tangled with the Kiowas, the Blackfeet, the Bloods, and others. Each time he'd been fortunate to escape with his scalp, and he wasn't eager to test his luck again.

Not that anyone would think to call him a coward. He'd proven his courage time and again, and in the process had acquired the Indian name of Grizzly Killer. Although he was tender in years, his exploits were already making the rounds of campfires in the Rockies and the Plains. If the stories continued to circulate, he reflected, one day he'd become as well known as Jim Bridger, Jed Smith, or his illustrious companion, the hardy mountain man called Shakespeare McNair.

"I've found plenty of beaver sign," that worthy man said. "We'll start setting out our traps tomorrow morning."

Nate squinted at the sun hovering an hour above the far horizon. "There's enough daylight left for us to set out a few before supper."

"Wisely and slow; they stumble that run fast."

"What?"

"I was quoting old William S.," Shakespeare disclosed.

"Oh," Nate said. He should have known. McNair's passion for the Bard of Avon was legendary among the trappers, and accounted for the mountain man's unusual sobriquet. Decades ago a fellow frontiersman had bestowed the title in jest, and it had stuck.

Now no one knew Shakespeare's true first name, and there wasn't a soul in the Rockies foolish enough to pry.

"Those who are tender in years are always in a great hurry to do this or that," Shakespeare commented. "The fire of youth hasn't yet turned to the ice of old age."

"Shakespeare again?"

"No, my own observation." Shakespeare turned to the southeast. "Let's go set up camp."

"Do you want me to go back after the elk?"

"No. It'll be miles away by now. We'll catch a few fish or shoot small game for our meal."

Nate followed dutifully. He still felt uneasy about the shot, but arguing with Shakespeare would be as productive as arguing with a rock. Surveying the landscape, he saw nothing out of the ordinary, and convinced himself he was letting his imagination get the better of him.

"Too bad we didn't bring Winona along," Shakespeare remarked. "That woman of yours sure can cook."

"You don't need to convince me," Nate said, and patted his stomach. His darling wife, a beautiful Shoshone, knew ways of preparing fabulous dishes from such common fare as buffalo, venison, and rabbit. Trained from childhood in the arts every Indian woman was required to know, Winona could sew expertly, do marvelous beadwork, ride a horse as competently as a warrior, and dress and tan buffalo and other hides. In his estimation, she was the perfect wife.

Once, he had considered marrying another. The thought unleashed a torrent of memories. Was it really only six months ago that he'd left New York City to join his Uncle Zeke on the frontier? At the time, forsaking his family, friends, and a promising job as an accountant had been an unnerving proposition, but nowhere near as hard to do as leaving behind the woman he'd loved, Adeline Van Buren.

But had he actually cared for Adeline in the depths of his heart, or only believed he did? Her beauty, wit, and wealth were enough to sway any man, and he'd fallen for her charms the first time they'd met. Few things in life had ever astonished him as much as when she reciprocated his affection. To tell the truth, he'd never felt worthy of her love. She was a goddess; he a lowly commoner. In recent days when he mused on their relationship, he consoled himself with the fact their marriage would never have worked out. She would have enslaved him to obey her every whim, and his resentment would eventually have boiled over and served to separate them.

Why did he bother thinking about Adeline anymore? Nate wondered. Now he had a wonderful wife, a woman he could treat as an equal, a woman he related to as a person instead of placing her on a pedestal, and he was blissfully, almost indecently happy. Why dwell on Adeline when he had Winona?

Was it because he felt so guilty about running off and leaving her without bothering to discuss his plans? Was it because he'd written letters promising to return to New York and wed her once he made his fortune?

His fortune!

Nate chuckled and shook his head at the foolish notions he'd once entertained. When Uncle Zeke had sent a letter promising to share "the greatest treasure in the world," Nate had naively assumed Zeke referred to gold or riches accumulated in the lucrative fur trade. He'd envisioned becoming as wealthy as Adeline's father and being able to support her in the extravagant manner to which she was accustomed. So off he'd gone to join Zeke.

Only later, as Ezekiel King lay dying, had Nate learned the nature of the treasure, a gift more precious than glittering ore or bags of money, the greatest gift a person could know: genuine freedom. The freedom to live as he pleased without having to account to others who considered themselves his betters. The freedom to let his conscience, his own inner light, be the sole determiner of his actions instead of the laws, rules, and regulations imposed by those who pompously sat in artificial positions of authority.

Freedom. Nate mentally savored the word, thinking of how much he had learned about the kind of life the Good Lord meant for people to live since coming to the wilderness. Ironic, wasn't it, that only by casting off the shackles of civilization and returning to the natural roots of humanity had he discovered the true meaning of existence?

"Is it a private joke or one you can share?"

The unexpected question brought Nate out of his reverie. "What?" he blurted out, and realized the frontiersman had stopped and was regarding him in obvious amusement. Nate likewise halted.

"What's so funny?"

"Oh. I was thinking about my past."

"Anyone under twenty hasn't had enough experience to have a past," Shakespeare said, moving on. "All they have are a few dozen memories."

"You're in a critical mood today," Nate remarked, trailing the older man.

"I get this way when I have the itch."

"You were bitten by a mosquito?"

"No," Shakespeare laughed. "I mean the itch to travel, to go off roaming by myself."

Shocked by the revelation, Nate nearly tripped over his own feet. "You plan to leave?"

"I've been thinking about it."

"What's your rush?"

"Rush? Here it is the first week in September already. We've been together pretty near two months. I wouldn't want to wear out my welcome."

"Nonsense. You're welcome to stay with us as long as you want," Nate said calmly, although secretly the prospect of his friend leaving filled him with dread. He'd grown to rely on the frontiersman's seasoned wisdom and flawless knowledge of the wildlife and people inhabiting the savage realm stretching between the Mississippi and the Pacific Ocean.

"I'd like to go see if my own cabin is still standing," Shakespeare mentioned.

"We can go together."

"You don't understand, Nate. Except for the rendezvous and an occasional trip to St. Louis, I'm not a great one for human company. Oh, I'll join up with a few friends from time to time to trap or hunt or whatever, but basically I like to be by my lonesome. Why do you think I was one of the very first white men to settle in the Rockies?"

Nate said nothing.

"Because I like my privacy. Out here a man can live without feeling crowded. I can walk for days without encountering another living soul, which certainly isn't the case back East. Too much of anything can be harmful, and that holds true for folks as well as food."

"Winona and I enjoy your company," Nate said gloomily.

"And I've liked staying with the two of you. I'm right fond of you both. But it's almost time for me to pull up stakes and get on with my life."

"We'll miss you."

"I haven't left yet," Shakespeare said, and smiled. "First I'll keep my promise to teach you all about trapping beaver, then I'll be on my way."

Nate stared out over the well-nigh limitless expanse of forest and mountains. "I don't know if we're ready to fend for ourselves yet."

"You are."

"How do you know?"

"Because I know both of you so well. Winona is a Shoshone; she can live off the land better than any white woman and most white men. You were a greenhorn when you first came out here with your uncle, but you've learned a lot since. I believe you have the makings of a man who will be remembered for years to come, just like Joe Walker."

"I'll never be as good as Walker," Nate responded, although he appreciated the compliment. Joseph Reddeford Walker, like Bridger, Smith, and McNair, was widely considered to be one of the best mountain men. Many rated him as *the* ablest mountaineer.

"Don't sell yourself short. No man can predict his destiny. We never know from one minute to another what the next moment will bring, especially out here where a man's life is at the mercy of circumstances he can't control."

They hiked onward in contemplative quiet until they arrived at a clearing bordered on the west by a bubbling spring and on the south by a large log. Tied to that log were their four horses.

"Since we'll be working along the stream anyway, why didn't we make camp there instead of a quarter of a mile away?" Nate absently inquired as he walked to his mare.

"Because waterways are a lot like roads. Everyone sticks near water when they're traveling in the wild. Indians and whites alike prefer to travel along the banks of streams and rivers where the going is easier and they can easily slake their thirst. If we camped near the stream we'd increase the likelihood of being discovered by Utes or Blackfeet," Shakespeare said, and gestured at the spring. "We're safer at this hideaway. I doubt whether even any Indians know about it, yet we're within easy walking distance of the stream. We can conduct our trapping operations in secrecy and not have to worry too much about being attacked."

Nate reached the mare and patted her neck. "Too much?"

"There's always that one in a million chance of Indians finding us, so don't let your guard down for an instant."

"I won't," Nate promised, propping his rifle between his legs while thinking of their arrival at the clearing an hour ago. They had immediately proceeded to the stream to check for beaver, not even bothering to remove their saddles. Shakespeare had once trapped the general area, five years ago, and knew the lay of the land well. Isolated and abundant with wildlife, the spot seemed ideal for the frontiersman to instruct Nate in the techniques of trapping. Nate began to unfasten the cinch.

"The reason so many trappers get killed is through sheer carelessness," Shakespeare went on in a talkative vein. "They forget to keep an eye on their surroundings and don't discover there are Indians about until it's too late. Study the ways of Nature. Animals are always wary, and we should be the same. You'll never see a squirrel lay down on the ground to take a nap since the critter knows it wouldn't last five minutes. Deer don't sleep out in the open, birds spend more time in trees than they do on the ground, and big fish stay in the deeper pools for the same reason. They're naturally wary."

Nate finished undoing the cinch and glanced at his grizzled teacher. "Don't fret about me. I have no intention of making Winona a widow so soon after we were married."

Shakespeare grinned, and had opened his mouth to reply when a deep growl rumbled from the surrounding forest.

Chapter Two

In a flash Nate pressed the Hawken to his shoulder and pivoted, spying the source of the growl at the edge of the trees to the north. He'd expected to see one of the fierce lords of the mountains, a beast capable of crushing a man's skull with a single swipe of its mighty paw, a mighty grizzly. Instead, to his relief, he saw a large black bear. The black variety seldom bothered humans; more often than not they fled at the sight of a trapper. He started to lower the rifle.

Shakespeare had spun at the sound, and now stood with his rifle held at waist height, staring at the bear.

"For a second there I thought we were in trouble," Nate commented, wondering why the bear didn't flee. The brute looked from one to the other as if perplexed. "Get out of here!" he shouted to drive it off.

The big black charged, dirt flying from under its claws, gaining speed with every stride, its powerful muscles rippling under its inky fur, its teeth exposed as it snarled.

Shocked, Nate instinctively raised the Hawken and fired. He heard the frontiersman's rifle discharge a heartbeat later, and the black bear reacted as if struck in the head with a heavy club. The beast sagged in midstride, its chin dropping to its chest, and collapsed, sliding a yard before lying motionless on the grass within six feet of Shakespeare.

"You won't need to go hunting for our supper after all."

Blood oozed from a pair of holes in the bear's head. Nate approached the beast cautiously in case a spark of life remained, his right hand resting on a flintlock. "Why did it come after us? I thought black bears usually leave people alone."

"Usually, but not always. This proves my point about staying alert. And never, ever, take anything for granted."

"You've convinced me," Nate said, tentatively prodding the bear with his left toe. Blood smeared onto the tip of his moccasin. He set to work reloading the Hawken.

"Tell you what. If you'll tend to the horses, I'll skin the bear and carve us a couple of juicy steaks. What do you say?"

"Sounds fair to me," Nate said, and finished reloading. He was amazed at how the frontiersman took every incident in stride. No matter how unexpected, or how violent, Shakespeare seldom became rattled. The man's composure was superb, and Nate wished he could be the same way.

For the next half hour few words were spoken as each man attended to his chores. Nate unsaddled the mare and Shakespeare's white horse, then removed the packs from their pack animals. He led all four to the spring to drink, and hobbled them so they could graze without straying off. One of the first sayings Nate learned after arriving in the mountains was the basic creed of horse tending: "It's better to count ribs than tracks." Which meant it was wiser to tie a horse at night and have the animal be hungry in the morning than let it wander off to gorge itself and be taken by an Indian. Many tribes were notorious horses stealers.

Next Nate went about gathering wood for the fire, carrying armloads of broken branches to the center of the clearing and forming convenient piles for later use. He got the blaze going, arranged his blanket near the fire so it would be warm when he retired, and went to help his companion.

Shakespeare was kneeling next to the carcass, artfully employing his twelve-inch butcher knife in removing the second choice cut of meat. "About done," he said.

Twilight had descended. The last, lingering rays of sunlights streaked the western sky. All around were birds singing their farewell chorus to the expiring day. Off in the distance a coyote howled.

Nate breathed deeply and smiled. Moments like this filled him with a joy at being alive, a joy he'd never experienced back in New York City.

"After we eat we'll cut up the rest of this bear and hang the meat to dry," Shakespeare said. "We don't want it lying around overnight. Wolves and such might get the notion to pay us a visit."

"Wolves don't bother humans very often."

"There you go again. What did I just tell you about taking things for granted? True, wolves ordinarily leave us alone. But if you run into a starving pack in the middle of winter, you'll find they're just like any other animal. They'll eat whatever they can catch."

"Have you ever given any thought to writing down all you've learned over the years?"

The frontiersman laughed. "Whatever for?"

"The people in the States have a great interest in anything written about the frontier. A factual book about your experiences would sell extremely well and make you a lot of money."

"I don't need a lot of money, and I'm not about to let others exploit my life to make their own easier."

"I don't understand."

Shakespeare looked up. "Everything I know I've learned the hard way. I didn't get these gray hairs by taking it easy and living in the lap of luxury. The way I see it, life is intended to be an education. Year by year we learn certain lessons and add to our knowledge, or else we don't learn a blessed thing and blunder on making the same mistakes over and over again. If I was to put down all I've learned on paper, I'd be depriving a lot of folks of the opportunity to learn life for themselves."

"I never thought of it that way," Nate said.

Standing, Shakespeare extended a dripping slab of meat. "I'm hungry. How about you?"

They walked to the fire and the frontiersman prepared their steaks. He prided himself on his cooking ability, and hovered over the simmering slabs until they were roasted to perfection.

Nate's mouth was watering by the time his steak was placed on the end of a sharpened stick and handed over. He used his knife both to cut off succulent strips and to cram the meat in his mouth. Grease dribbled over his lower lip and down his chin, but he didn't care. He savored every bite, relishing the tangy taste and the warm sensation in his stomach. The finest steak in New York couldn't begin to compare to a slice of buffalo, bear, or deer meat prepared over an open fire high in the Rocky Mountains. There was an indescribable quality about such crude fare that satisfied the appetite like no other food.

"Tomorrow we begin educating you on the ways of the beaver," Shakespeare said between chomps.

"I'm looking forward to it," Nate said. "Was my Uncle Zeke a good trapper?"

"Your uncle was talented in everything he tried. The man had a knack, and I've seen evidence of the same trait in you."

Nate started to take another bite, then paused. "I just realized I've never written my dad to tell him Zeke died. He'd want to know."

"Were they close?"

"When they were younger. But they drifted apart after Zeke decided to leave for the frontier. My dad could never understand why Zeke wanted to go."

"How did he feel about you leaving?"

"I imagine he felt the same way."

Shakespeare lowered his steak. "Didn't you talk it over with him before you left?"

"I wrote him a letter."

"Were you afraid he'd try to stop you?"

"Yes," Nate confessed. "None of my family would have accepted the idea. They'd have badgered me mercilessly until I changed my mind. As it is, they probably despise me now."

"Never underestimate the love of your kin."

"I know my family better than you do. Why, my father forbade us from ever mentioning Zeke's name in the house. His own brother!"

"Pride is a bitter pill to swallow."

"What do you mean?"

"Your father probably knows he made a mistake and he's too proud to admit it. He won't let anyone talk about Zeke because he doesn't want to be reminded of . . ." Shakespeare paused, cocking his head.

"What is it?"

"Listen."

Nate did, but heard only the sounds of wildlife and the whisper of the breeze.

"Do you hear it?"

"Hear what?"

"The horse."

Again Nate strained his ears, and this time he detected the faint drumming of pounding hooves. He stood, swiveling in the direction of the sound, to the southwest, and gazed into the gloomy woods.

"Whoever it is must be a fool or bent on committing suicide," Shakespeare said, standing. "It's too dark to be riding a horse at a full gallop in the forest."

"I've done it," Nate commented, recalling his recent encounter with a Ute war party. He suddenly realized he was still holding the steak, and placed the meat on the grass so he could grab his rifle.

The pounding became louder and louder, and it was obvious the rider would pass very close to their camp.

"Don't shoot until we see who it is."

"I won't," Nate said. He heard the crack of a limb and the crunching of underbrush, and leaned forward to peer intently into the darkness. At the limit of his vision he perceived movement and distinguished the outline of a horse and rider heading eastward.

In a matter of seconds the newcomer was 20 yards south of the camp and still galloping recklessly when the man happened to glance to his left and spied the fire. His head snapped up and he hauled on the reins.

"It's a white man," Shakespeare said.

How could he tell? Nate wondered. *He* couldn't perceive any of the rider's features beyond noting the man wore buckskins.

"Hello!" the newcomer cried, and rode toward them. "Please don't fire. I mean you no harm."

Nate kept the Hawken handy just in case. He glanced at Shakespeare, who had also taken the precaution of grabbing his rifle, and placed his thumb on the hammer.

"Come closer, stranger," the frontiersman announced.

"Thank you." The man came to the edge of the clearing and stopped. He wore the typical attire of a mountaineer: buckskins, moccasins, and a wool cap. The inevitable bullet pouch and powder horn crisscrossed his chest. A shock of blond hair rimmed a rugged face dominated by blue eyes. "I didn't think there was another trapper within a hundred miles of here," he remarked happily.

"Do you have a name?" Shakespeare asked.

"Thaddeus Baxter at your service, sir. And who might you be?"

"Shakespeare McNair, and this here is Nate King," the frontiersman said with a nod of his head.

Baxter focused on Nate. "Aren't you the one they call Grizzly Killer? The same one who killed the rogue Canadian known as the Giant during the rendezvous?"

"I am."

"I thought I recognized the two of you," Baxter said, grinning. "The Good Lord has smiled on me."

"How is it you know us?" Shakespeare asked.

"I was at the rendezvous. Both of you were pointed out to me by an acquaintance, but we were never introduced."

"Why don't you climb on down? You're welcome to share our supper if you're hungry," Shakespeare said.

"Thank you," Baxter replied, riding closer before he dismounted and stepped to the fire. "I couldn't eat a bite right now, not after what I've been through."

"Mind telling us why you were riding your horse into the ground?"

"Blackfeet," Baxter said.

"This far south?"

"I couldn't believe it myself," Baxter stated. "I imagine it's a war party down here to raid the Utes."

"What happened?" Nate prompted.

"My own camp is about four miles from here. An hour or so before sunset I was skinning a couple of beaver I'd caught, whistling to myself without a care in the world, when my pack animal whinnied and I looked up to find a dozen or more Blackfeet creeping toward me."

"That was your shot we heard earlier," Shakespeare deduced.

"Must have been. I grabbed my rifle and fired once, killing one of the bastards, but then the rest swarmed on me and it was all I could do to fight them off using my rifle like a club," Baxter replied. "I think they were trying to take me alive. Otherwise I'd be dead right now."

"But you got away," the frontiersman said.

"Barely. My rifle was torn from my hands just as I broke loose and ran into the forest. They chased me, but I hid, then circled back to my camp. There was one warrior guarding my horses, so I knocked him on the head and cut out. Unfortunately, several others showed up and I had to leave without my pack animal and all my supplies."

"And here you are," Nate stated.

Baxter laughed lightly. "By pure chance. I might have kept going all the way to St. Louis if I hadn't spotted your camp. Without traps and a rifle, there's no sense in trapping beaver."

"We can go after your belongings in the morning," Shakespeare offered.

"And get youselves killed on my account? No, sir.

There's too many of them."

Nate gazed at the foreboding forest. "Were they after you?"

"No. They fired a few arrows but didn't give chase."

"Strange," Shakespeare said. "Blackfeet are the most persistent devils I know."

"I was surprised too," Baxter said. "Even on foot they'll go after a mounted man."

"They didn't have any horses?" Nate asked.

"Just my pack animal."

Shakespeare turned to his protégé. "Quite often the Blackfeet send out war parties on foot. They believe they can move quieter in enemy territory. I've also heard tell the warriors are expected to steal the mounts they need to ride back to their village."

"And they are some of the best horse thieves around," Baxter added.

Again Nate surveyed the woods. "What if they sent a warrior after you on your pack animal?"

"He would never catch me. My pack animal is the slowest critter this side of the Divide." Baxter chuckled. "Besides, no one in their right mind would ride as fast as I did."

"Then we should be safe here," Nate concluded.

"I didn't lead the Blackfeet to you, if that's what you're thinking," Baxter said.

Shakespeare took his seat and picked up his bear steak. "You're welcome to spend the night with us, Thaddeus."

"I'd be in your debt."

"Nonsense. It's the least we can do for a fellow trapper. There are few enough of us living in the wilderness as it is. We must help each other out when the need arises or we're no better than the animals we contend with every day."

Baxter smiled gratefully. "Thank you."

Retrieving his steak, Nate sat down and took a bite of the warm meat. While he shared Shakespeare's sentiments on helping someone in need, he entertained grave reservations about staying to trap the stream. The Blackfeet were too close for comfort, but he wasn't about to question Shakespeare's judgment. He'd see their labors through to the end, and just pray the end wasn't his own.

Chapter Three

Bright morning sunshine and invigorating, crisp mountain air served to dispel Nate's doubts of the night before. He was eager to learn the life of a free trapper, and although a slight uneasiness gnawed at the back of his mind, he was the first one done eating breakfast and raring to go. "Ready when you are," he announced after consuming several strips of dried buffalo meat.

"Hold your horses," Shakespeare said with a grin. "I'll be done in a minute." He looked at their new acquaintance, who was chewing hungrily on a piece of raw bear meat. "You can cook as much as you like."

"This is fine," Baxter said. "I usually eat light in the morning."

Shakespeare stared at the makeshift rack they'd constructed before retiring, using stout branches and rope, and noted with satisfaction the thin slices of flesh aligned side by side, well out of the reach of most predators. "By this afternoon we'll have more jerked meat than we can possibly use. If you're still keen on going, take whatever you need."

"I haven't quite made up my mind about leaving."

Nate placed his rifle stock on the ground and idly leaned on the barrel, reviewing what they'd learned of Baxter's past while sitting around the fire and conversing until after midnight.

Thaddeus Baxter hailed from Ohio. Thirty-one years old, he had a wife and two children eagerly awaiting his return. Eighteen months ago he'd left his home to travel beyond the mighty Mississippi, his head filled with notions of making it rich in the fur trade. There were many tales of those who had, most prominent of them all being John Jacob Astor.

Astor emmigrated to America from Germany at the age of twenty, went into the fur business shortly thereafter, had the audacity born of firm conviction to start his own company, and wound up earning the newspaper-bestowed title of "the richest man in the country." Many a young man, on reading of Astor's phenomenal success, bid his loved ones a hopefully temporary good-bye and headed for the prime beaver grounds in the Rocky Mountains. For every one hundred who went, perhaps a dozen were lucky enough to live to see the States again, and of that dozen none acquired great wealth.

Nate felt sympathy for the Ohioan, based on his own former dream of becoming incredibly rich. The thought of Baxter's family, though, troubled him. What would happen to them if the man died? Baxter had sent back letters with men heading homeward, but letters were no substitute for the loving presence of a husband and a father. And eighteen months was a long separation. In Nate's estimation, leaving a wife and children was far worse than leaving parents and siblings.

"I have a proposal to make," Baxter said.

"Let's hear it," Shakespeare responded.

"After a year and a half of one mishap after

another, I'm beginning to think I made a mistake. My first season trapping I collected over two hundred pelts—"

"Not bad," Shakespeare said, interrupting.

"And lost them all when I tried to cross a flooded river and the canoe capsized," Baxter went on. "My second season I fared better and took in three hundred and fifty pelts. Half the money I sent to my family, and the rest I used to outfit myself and two good men with enough traps and supplies to guarantee success." He frowned. "We'd taken over eight hundred pelts when we were attacked by Bloods. My friends were killed and I barely escaped with my life."

Nate listened intently. He'd heard similar stories of woe before. The harsh economic realities of trapping had ruined many a trapper.

For an initial investment of several hundred dollars, including the expenses of a mount, rifle, ammunition, pistols, a knife and hatchet, clothing, and provisions, a trapper stood to make a hefty profit. There were two trapping seasons each year in which the trapper could ply his trade, the spring and fall seasons. The first began when winter's ice started to break up and went on until early summer, when the quality of beaver fur declined due to the heat. The hotter it became, the thinner the fur. Then came the second season in late August or early September, lasting until the ponds and streams iced over. During each season a skilled trapper could accumulate hundreds of pelts. By rendezvous time, this translated into an average of two thousand dollars, a huge sum by any standard. After several years, a prudent trapper could save quite a hoard.

Or so it seemed on paper to men back East who had no idea of the realities of the trapping trade. They didn't know, for instance, that the Rocky Mountain Fur Company enjoyed a virtual monopoly of the trading activities in the Rockies. The Company paid two to four dollars for beaver pelts at the rendezvous, then resold them for eight dollars in St. Louis. And since the rendezvous was the only market for the trappers' furs, there was nothing that could be done to change the situation.

To make matters worse, the suppliers at the rendezvous were invariably in cahoots with the Fur Company. They overpriced their goods by as much as 2000 percent, and the trappers were forced to buy such inflated supplies or go without. In effect, the heads of the company and the suppliers grew rich at the trappers' expense.

Then why am I here? Nate asked himself. Undoubtedly because even with all the financial drawbacks and the hardships of living off the land, the life of a mountaineer offered a consolation few other ways of living could: genuine freedom. He could do as he pleased when he pleased. No one was standing over his shoulder, goading him to work harder or faster. No one could impose on him in any respect. He was the master of his own destiny, and he loved it.

"I'm tired of wasting my time and energy," Baxter was saying. "And I've been away from my family so long that my own children might not recognize me." He paused. "I was hoping you'd see fit to let me trap with you for a month. Then I'll take my fair share of the pelts and head for St. Louis. I should be able to find a buyer there who will offer a bit more than the Rocky Mountain Fur Company representatives. If I'm lucky, I'll head for Ohio with four or five hundred dollars in my pocket. What do you say?"

Shakespeare pursed his lips and stroked his beard, then looked at Nate. "What do you think?"

"I don't mind if you don't."

Baxter anxiously leaned toward the fontiersman. "Please, McNair. Your kindness would mean so much to me. I don't want to go home with empty pockets. I don't want to let my loved ones down entirely." He sighed. "I feel as if I'm a monumental failure, and this is my chance to redeem myself."

"No man is a failure if he's still breathing," Shakespeare said solemnly.

"Will you let me stay?"

"Nate has already said he has no objections, and it's his decision that counts. I'm here to teach him how to trap, nothing more. I have no intention of trapping for myself, and there's more than enough beaver hereabouts to satisfy the needs of two men."

"Then I can stay?" Baxter inquired eagerly.

"So long as you uphold your end of the work."

Baxter stood, stepped over to the frontiersman, and vigorously pumped Shakespeare's right hand. "I can never thank you enough for your Christian generosity."

"Actually, I have an ulterior motive."

"You do?"

"Yes. You're an experienced trapper, so you can help me teach Nate the tricks of the trade. With both of us instructing him, he'll learn that much quicker and I can leave that much sooner."

Nate pretended to be interested in a hawk circling to the north so neither of them would see his crest-fallen expression. Shakespeare was inordinately excited about departing. After all they had been through, nearly losing their lives time and again, after traveling so many miles together and growing so close, he was upset that Shakespeare wanted to abruptly sever their ties.

"Where are you going?" Baxter asked.

"Wherever the wind takes me."

"Will you ever visit Ohio?"

A spontaneous laugh burst from the mountain man's lips. "Never. I've had my full of civilization. The farthest east I'll ever go is St. Louis. Why do you ask?"

"I'd like to repay you some day for your kindness."

"You can repay me by watching your hair on the way east. A lone white man is at the mercy of Fate out here."

Baxter squared his shoulders. "I'll trust in the Lord to see me safely through."

For a moment Shakespeare sat perfectly still. He stared off into the distance, then pried a fingernail between two teeth to remove a wad of food. "I take it you're a Christian?"

"A Presbyterian," Baxter stated proudly.

"Is that a fact?" Shakespeare responded. "Most trappers are an irreligious lot. In all my years of living in the mountains, I've only known two Christians, and they are as different as night and day."

"Who might they be?"

"One is Jed Smith. He's the best trapper alive and the most consistent Christian I've ever met. Of course, he's also a bit inflexible at times. Always believes he knows the best way to do things and won't listen to anyone else. But he'll go out of his way to help a person in trouble."

"And who is the other man?"

"Old Bill Williams. He totes a bible everywhere he goes and claims the Lord speaks to him personally every night. Lives by himself way back in the Rockies and likes it that way. Can't stand the company of others and wouldn't go out of his way to save a dying baby."

"Aren't you being unfair?"

"No. I know Williams as well as anyone. And I suspect the rumors about him are true."

"What rumors?"

"Old Bill is partial to eating human flesh."

Baxter grimaced. "Not another one."

"You've heard about Crazy George?"

"He was the talk of the rendezvous. I understand

one of you killed him."

"I did."

"Wasn't he a friend of yours?"

"One of the best I ever had."

Nate glanced at Shakespeare, memories of that terrible night etched indelibly in his mind. Crazy George had joined a band of cutthroats and taken to murdering trappers while they slept to steal their money. Eventually Shakespeare had confronted the maniac and been forced to kill him. "We should head on out," Nate suggested.

"I agree," Shakespeare declared, rising abruptly. "Grab your equipment and let's go find us some beaver."

Five minutes later they were hiking toward the stream. Nate and Baxter carried sacks containing six traps apiece and wooden boxes containing the bait they would need. Once at the water they marched upstream until they discovered a beaver dam, where they halted on the west bank.

"Now pay close attention," Shakespeare directed Nate. "If you hope to make a living as a free trapper, this is how you will do it." He took Nate's sack and removed one of the Newhouse traps, so named for the man who manufactured them in New York. "Find us a nice, long stick."

Eagerly Nate complied, his sorrow at soon being left to fend for himself replaced by unrestrained zeal of learning the intricate details of his desired craft. He used his knife to chop off a branch three feet long. "Will this do?" he asked as he returned.

"It will do nicely. Did you bring your hatchet?"

Nate's mouth dropped at his oversight. "No. I forgot."

"You can use mine," Baxter said, and produced one from behind his back.

"First rule," Shakespeare said. "Always take all the equipment you will need."

"I'll remember next time," Nate promised.

"Okay. Now follow me." The frontiersman waded slowly into the water.

Tentatively placing his left foot in, Nate shivered when the ice-cold water immediately soaked his moccasins and enveloped his lower leg in its frigid grip.

Shakespeare noticed and chuckled. "If you can't tolerate a little cold, this is no business for you. The water in these mountain streams is never warm, not even in the summer, because most of it is snow runoff."

"I'm fine," Nate said.

"Good. Now let's attend to business." Shakespeare extended the trap. "Haven't you forgotten something?"

"No," Nate replied uncertainly.

"Second rule. Always cock your trap before you enter the water."

Only then did Nate realize the trap wasn't set. "Why didn't you have me do it sooner?"

"We learn best when we learn from our mistakes. This way you'll remember the next time," Shakespeare said, and moved closer to the bank. "Baxter, would you do the honors?"

"Gladly." The Ohioan took the Newhouse, placed it on the ground, and proceeded to stand on the leaf springs so the jaws would fall flat. He carefully adjusted the trigger and the disk until the proper tension existed, then quickly lifted first one foot, then the other. Lifting the trap by the edge of a leaf spring, he gave it to the frontiersman.

"Rule number three. Never stick your fingers or thumbs between the jaws unless you no longer have any use for them."

"I knew a man who once lost two fingers in a trap," Baxter mentioned.

"Now comes the hard part," Shakespeare said,

studying the water near the bank. He moved a few feet and pointed at a flat spot six inches below the surface. "You want to set the trap in place without disturbing the trigger. It's important that the surface be no higher than a hand width above the disk."

"Why?" Nate inquired.

"Because beavers aren't storks. They have short, stubby legs, and the trap works best if they step right on the disk. If you place it lower, they'll probably swim right over it. Here. You put it down."

Nate complied, doing so gingerly, wary of the trap accidentally snapping shut. "Now what?"

"Take the stick and insert it through the loop at the end of the chain, then pound it into the stream bed."

Again Nate obeyed, but as he went to swing the hatchet an admonition stopped him.

"Not yet. Pull the chain as far as it will go. The purpose is to drown the beaver before it can gnaw off its foot."

"They do that?"

"Every now and then. Even beaver like to live."

The disclosure bothered Nate. He envisioned a helpless beaver caught in his trap, its lungs on fire, furiously chewing on its own leg to gain freedom.

"What are you waiting for?"

"Nothing," Nate said, and did as he'd been told. Straightening, he saw the frontiersman clambering onto the bank and walked toward him. "What's next?"

"Climb on out."

Happy to quit the water, Nate joined his companions. He leaned down and wrung water from his pants.

Shakespeare pointed at the spot where Nate had deposited the rifle and bait box. "Grab your box, then get a twig six to eight inches long. Make certain the twig has leaves on one end."

Once again Nate obeyed. The small wooden box contained the musky secretion taken from several dead beavers. He'd purchased it at the rendezvous from an elderly trapper.

"Now dip the leaves in the medicine," Shakespeare said.

Nate nodded. "Medicine" was the word trappers used to describe the musk because it possessed medicinal properties. A salve made of beaver oil and castoreum, the gummy, yellow musk, worked wonders on open wounds, easing the pain and drawing out the swelling. Nate had never used the salve himself, but he'd heard many mountaineers swear by its curative properties. He opened the box and dabbed the leaves in the gum.

"That's enough. Now stick the bottom of the twig in the bank so that the leaves hang about six inches above the trap."

Dropping to one knee, Nate bent over and inserted the twig into the soft earth until he was satisfied the twig would hold fast. He stood and waited further instructions.

"Congratulations," Shakespeare said with a grin. "You've set your first beaver trap. Any beaver coming within two or three hundred yards of the medicine will smell the odor and swim over to emit some of its own musk on the spot. When the critter goes to climb out, its leg will get caught in the trap. Then it's only a matter of time before the animal drowns."

"Or chews its leg off," Nate said distastefully.

The corners of the frontiersman's eyes crinkled. "If you check your traps twice a day, as you should, any beavers you catch won't have time to gnaw off their legs. Most trappers are too lazy for their own good and only check their traps at sunup, so it's not surprising they lose a goodly number of animals."

"I'll check mine twice a day," Nate promised. The

last thing he wanted was to inflict needless suffering on poor animals whose only offense against man was the fact they were covered with prime fur.

Shakespeare rubbed his hands together. "Let's set up the rest of these traps. We can be done by noon and head back to camp for some more of that bear meat."

"Sounds good to me," Baxter said.

Along the stream they went, choosing spots to place traps with deliberate care, traveling several miles to the north before the last of the Newhouses waited under the water for an unsuspecting beaver.

Nate enjoyed laying the traps. He became accustomed to the cold water, at least to the point that the temperature didn't bother him. He saw many big fish swimming unconcernedly past as he labored, and resolved to try his hand at catching several for supper. Birds chirped in the deciduous trees and the pines, and small creatures such as squirrels, rabbits, and chipmunks were everywhere. The vibrant pulse of Nature stirred his soul, and he savored the experience of being alive.

When they turned their steps toward their camp, Baxter gave Nate a friendly clap on the back. "Thanks again for letting me stay. I can tell this valley is prime beaver territory, and I should take back enough furs to reap a tidy profit."

"I'm glad I could help."

They retraced their route eagerly, spurred by healthy appetites, and conversed about the trapping trade in general. Engrossed in their discussion, none of them paid much attention to their surroundings until they were almost to the edge of the clearing.

Nate was the first to look up and discover their meat being pilfered from the rack, and his breath caught in his throat at sight of the culprit.

For there, its wicked mouth crammed with strips of flesh, stood a monster grizzly.

Chapter Four

If no one had uttered a sound, the bear might have kept on eating and peaceably departed after consuming its full. But such wasn't to be the case.

"A grizzly!" Baxter blurted out.

At the sound of a human voice the monster growled and spun toward them, twelve hundred pounds of muscle and sinew poised to hurtle forward. A yellowish-brown coat distinguished by individual white-tipped hairs gave the giant its grizzled aspect. Bulging above the beast's massive shoulders was the breed's distinctive hump. Brutish, concave features that could inspire terror in whites and Indians alike were twisted in primal hatred.

"Don't say another word," Shakespeare whispered. "Stand perfectly still and maybe it won't attack. They have pitiful eyesight and the wind is blowing in our faces."

Nate gripped his Hawken until his knuckles turned white. By some strange quirk of Fate, he seemed to have a knack for encountering grizzlies. Twice since crossing the Mississippi he'd been attacked by the terrible beasts, and twice he'd barely escaped with his life.

The grizzly raised its head and sniffed loudly, then took a lumbering stride forward.

"Don't move," Shakespeare reiterated.

The temptation to flee was hard to resist. Nate knew a grizzly could lope as rapidly as a horse when the need arose, and he naturally wanted to get as far from the monster as swiftly as he could. With unblinking eyes he watched the giant, waiting for the animal to make up its mind whether to attack or not. He didn't have long to wait.

A tremendous, rumbling challenge erupted from the grizzly's throat, and suddenly it charged.

"Scatter!" Shakespeare shouted, and ran to the left.

Nate needed no urging. He sprinted to the right, weaving among the trees, while looking over his shoulder to ascertain the fate of his fellows. Shakespeare covered the ground at a remarkably spry pace, but Baxter wasn't faring so well.

The Ohioan traveled ten yards to the east, then realized the bear was coming after him. Panicked, he slanted toward an oak tree and grasped desperately at a low-hanging limb.

Maintaining a consistent, moderate speed, not bothering to go all out, the bear closed on the blond trapper.

Nate slowed, staring at the tableau. If Baxter reached the sanctuary of the higher branches, the bear would never be able to get him. Adult grizzlies, due to their great weight, were incapable of climbing trees. And since the brute was not running as fast as it could, he gathered it merely meant to drive them from the meat and wasn't motivated by bestial bloodlust. Once the trapper was in the clear, the bear would probably return to the rack. It was comforting to know that not all encounters with grizzlies had to end in violence.

Thaddeux Baxter unexpectedly slipped. He had managed to climb onto the bottom limb, and was trying to pull himself up onto a higher one when his left hand gave way, and the next moment he fell onto the ground on his back. There was no time to try again.

The grizzly had only 20 feet to cover. Whether it originally intended to slay them or not, such easy prey aroused all of its predatory instincts and it snarled to freeze its prey in place.

Instantly Nate whirled and dashed to Baxter's aid. The man didn't stand a prayer without help. He saw Shakespeare doing the same, and shouted to draw the grizzly's attention. "Bear! Try me, you flea-ridden brute!"

Halting, the grizzly wheeled in the direction of the shout and snorted.

Baxter was clawing at his pistol.

Whipping the rifle to his shoulder, Nate hoped the bear would flee before he squeezed the trigger. Single shots seldom dispatched a grizzly; the ball only served to drive them into an insane rage. Once he fired, the battle would be joined.

The bear took a few steps toward the onrushing human, then stopped as if confused.

"Run, damn you!" Nate yelled, and saw Baxter level the flintlock.

A heartbeat later the pistol discharged.

Struck near the ear, the grizzly lurched to the left, shaking its enormous head vigorously. It recovered in seconds, spun, and bore down on the trapper.

Baxter, still on his back, scrambled on his elbows in a frantic effort to get behind the trunk.

Nate had to shoot on the run. The bear was almost upon the trapper when Nate took a hasty bead on its left eye, cocked the hammer, and squeezed the trigger. The booming of the rifle seemed to have no effect on the carnivore except to provide it with a new outlet for its fury.

Spinning with astonishing agility, the grizzly opened its mouth wide and made straight for the presumptuous human.

Reloading or running was out of the question. Nate perceived the bear would be on him before he could do either, so he let the rifle fall and drew both pistols. Extending both arms, he pointed both barrels at the creature's head, waited until 15 feet separated them, and fired both guns.

The twin balls smacked into the grizzly's forehead and jerked the huge head backwards. Its front legs buckled and it sprawled forward, sliding several feet and stopping.

Elated, Nate believed he'd slain the brute, until it abruptly heaved erect and stood swaying from side to side, blood pouring from a wound over its right eye. He backpedaled, debating whether to try to reload or seek the safety of a tree.

Growling horribly, the grizzly shuffled in for the kill.

Nate bumped into a trunk, frantically stuck both pistols under his belt, and leaped for a limb overhead.

The bear bounded the final ten feet.

His body tingling in anticipation of being torn to shreds, Nate's hands closed on the limb and he wrenched his body upward in a tight arc, his legs sailing over a higher branch at the apex of his swing. Bending his knees, he looped his calves over the branch and snapped his body upward. An intense stinging sensation lanced across his left shoulder blade, and then he was perched on the limb, momentarily safe. A glance below showed him the grizzly in the act of standing. He spied another limb above him and to his left, and he vaulted from his perch. Something tugged at his right moccasin, throwing him off balance, and even as his hand wrapped around the limb his body fell sideways. Fear rippled through every fiber of his being in that terrible moment of dismaying comprehension that he would plummet to the earth. The bear! his mind shrieked. The bear will get you!

Nate smacked into a lower branch and inadvertently somersaulted onto the ground with a bone-jarring crash. Dazed, he struggled to rise, aware of a snarling form towering above him. Vaguely he heard a shot, and then something hit his head with enough force to shatter a boulder and his consciousness swirled madly before being sucked into an inky, ethereal void.

Somewhere, someone groaned.

Belatedly, Nate realized he was the one doing the groaning, and felt his awareness returning, felt life flow along his arms and legs, and felt the most awful, painful headache he'd ever known. His thoughts shifted and danced, and for a few minutes he couldn't concentrate.

"He's coming around," someone said.

"At last," stated someone else.

Both voices were familiar, and Nate knew he should be able to identify them, but his sluggish mind refused to cooperate. He blinked, and promptly regretted the movement. Dazzling, hurting light made him wince and recoil in agony.

"Take it easy, Nate. Lie still."

A gentle hand touched his shoulder, and suddenly Nate recognized the speaker. "Shakespeare?" he croaked.

"One and the same."

"I'm here too," added the first man.

"Baxter?" Nate blinked again, then squinted, his head throbbing. He licked his dry lips, peering at a bright blue sky, and saw the heads of both men materialize above him.

"Don't try to sit up," Shakespeare warned.

"What happened?" Nate asked, gradually regaining mental control. "The bear—"

"Is dead," Shakespeare finished. "You don't need to worry about him."

"I can't remember what happened," Nate said. "Did you kill it?"

"I shot last, but the thing was already dead on its feet," Shakespeare disclosed.

"Then what hit me?"

"The grizzly. It fell on top of you."

Baxter nodded. "We had to use the horses to haul the body off of you. We were afraid we'd find you dead, crushed or suffocated."

"You were fortunate, son," Shakespeare said.

Bewildered, trying to recall the events, Nate saw the sun out of the corner of his left eye. The golden orb hung low over the horizon. "I must have been out eight or nine hours. The sun is setting."

"The sun is rising," Shakespeare corrected him.

"What?"

Again Baxter nodded. "You were unconscious yesterday afternoon and all of last night. We took turns watching over you. McNair wasn't able to sleep a wink."

"It's morning?" Nate declared, incredulous at the news. He lifted his right hand and touched his forehead. "How bad is the wound?"

"You were cut on the shoulder blade and nicked on the foot, but you haven't lost much blood," the frontiersman responded.

"Why does my head ache so badly?"

"You were trying to get up when the bear went

down. Your head took the brunt of its weight," Shakespeare said, and grinned. "Your head must be as hard as iron."

"It doesn't feel like iron," Nate said. "It feels like mush."

"Which is why you will lie under your blankets for another day, at least."

Lowering his chin, Nate saw his blankets were indeed draped neatly over his body almost to his neck. "What about the beaver?"

"Thaddeus and I will take care of them," Shakespeare said. "We've already caught four."

The man from Ohio placed his hand on Nate's left arm. "I need to thank you again. If not for your intervention, the grizzly would have killed me. I've never seen anyone stand up to one of those beasts like you did. No wonder they call you Grizzly Killer."

"I'd rather be known as Sparrow Killer," Nate said sincerely.

Both Shakespeare and Baxter laughed.

"This makes three of those brutes you've killed," Shakespeare said after a bit. "Very few trappers have killed more than you. Most have the good sense to run like hell when they see one."

Again they laughed.

Nate tried to grin, but the simple movement increased the agony in his head. The pounding in his temples drowned out all other sound, and he closed his eyes, intending to rest for a minute. To his amazement, when next his lids pried apart there were stars dotting the firmament. "It's night," he blurted.

"Well, look who is awake," said Shakespeare, who was still seated in the same spot.

"Where's Thaddeus?"

"Sleeping. It's my turn to keep an eye on you."

"How late is it?"

"I don't know exactly. After midnight."

A growling in Nate's stomach reminded him he

hadn't eaten in ages. "I could use some food."

"The fire is going strong. I'll make you soup or coffee or both."

"I'd like something more substantial."

"Not yet. No solid foods until tomorrow."

"Why not?"

"When someone has been severely injured, eating solid foods can make them worse. It puts a strain on the body. So if you want food, I'll prepare bear stew."

"Did the grizzly leave enough meat to last us a while?"

"No. But there was enough meat *on* the grizzly to last for weeks."

"You carved him up?"

"Can't let prime flesh go to waste, now can we? Would you care for some stew?"

Nate smiled at the notion of consuming the bear responsible for his condition. "I'd love some."

"Then try to stay awake until I'm done," Shakespeare said, and moved off.

A cool breeze caressed Nate's brow and he savored the sensation. If there was one lesson he'd learned living in the wilderness, it was to never take life for granted. A person never knew when he might be killed by a freak mishap. All it took was a single accident, a chance encounter with a bear, a panther, or hostile Indians, to send a hapless soul into eternity.

Back in the cities the situation was different. The people were spared from the harsh reality of ever-present death by having their needs supplied at the mere exchange of money. Food, clothing, and shelter were theirs for a few coins. They didn't need to worry about starving if they couldn't track game, or going naked if they couldn't make their own clothes, or sleeping on the hard ground if they couldn't build a cabin or lodge. In a sense, they were denied certain basic experiences all persons should know if they were to truly understand the value of existence.

Was that proper? Nate asked himself. If men and women were denied the realities of life, what was left? The illusions? Did some people prefer living in the cities over the country because they preferred illusions to reality? If so, what did it say about the mental state of those who shunned the truth?

Sleepiness assailed Nate's senses and he struggled to stay alert. Rumblings in his stomach gave him the resolve necessary. He was famished, and his mouth watered at the thought of the stew his friend was preparing. He heard the pad of footsteps and looked up, expecting the frontiersman.

Instead, the Ohioan appeared.

"How are you feeling?"

"As well as can be expected. I was told you were sleeping."

"I can't seem to doze off for more than a couple of hours at a time. I'm too excited about the prospect of returning to my family." Baxter took a seat at Nate's right. "McNair told me you're married."

"Yes."

"To a Shoshone?" Baxter said.

"What's wrong with that?"

"Nothing. Nothing at all. I was surprised to hear it, is all. Most trappers take an Indian woman for a few months or even a year, but very few bother to marry them. Why did you?"

"I love her."

"You weren't motivated by religious principles?"

"No."

"Do you believe, Nate King?"

"Believe what?"

"In the Lord?"

"I believe there is a God, but I have no idea whether . . ." Nate abruptly ceased speaking when a strident chorus of piercing howls erupted from the nearby forest.

Chapter Five

"Wolves," Baxter declared, rising and drawing his flintlock.

Alarmed, his heart beating faster, Nate managed to prop himself on his elbows and glanced around. The light from the campfire illuminated the horses standing near the spring, their heads up, their nostrils flaring and their ears cocked. An encircling ring of murky vegetation enclosed their island of comforting warmth.

Shakespeare was in the act of chopping bear meat into a tin pan. He promptly placed the meat on the ground and grabbed his rifle.

The howling came from the north and west, a wavering, primitive carol that rose and fell in volume, attaining a crescendo of clamorous harmony only to drop to plaintive wails seconds later.

"Will they attack?" Baxter called out.

"I don't think so," Shakespeare answered. "They smell the bear meat. If their bellies were empty, they'd sneak up on us without a sound."

Nate hoped the mountain man was correct. In his

condition he wouldn't be able to fend off an ornery mosquito, let alone a pack of wolves. The nerve-racking minutes dragged past, with phantom shadows moving about in the undergrowth and their eerie cries wafting to the heavens.

"Why won't they go?" Baxter asked nervously.

Suddenly a large wolf materialized at the very edge of the trees, its eyes reflecting the firelight and glowing an unearthly red, its teeth exposed in a seeming canine grin. After calmly gazing from one man to another, the gray wolf at last whirled and melted into the night and with his departure the howling immediately stopped.

"Thank God," Baxter said.

"That must have been the leader," Shakespeare speculated.

"Why did he stare at us?" Baxter inquired.

"Curiosity. Maybe he wanted to get a good whiff of our scent."

"Why?"

The frontiersman knelt by the fire. "Thaddeus, do I look like a wolf to you?"

"Of course not."

"Then don't expect me to be able to think exactly like a wolf. I may know the animals of the Rockies better than most, but no matter how close a man gets to Nature, he never becomes a complete part of it. There is a quality about a man that forever separates him from the animal kingdom."

"His soul."

"And his will. Never forget the human will," Shakespeare said, and launched into a quote from his favorite author. " 'Tis in ourselves that we are thus or thus. Our bodies are gardens; to the which our wills are gardeners: so that if we will plant nettles or sow lettuce, set hyssop and weed up thyme, supply it with one gender of herbs or distract it with many, either to have it sterile with idleness or manured with industry, why, the power and corrigible authority of this lies in our wills. If the balance of our lives had not one scale of reason to poise another of sensuality, the blood and baseness of our natures would conduct us to most preposterous conclusions."

"I'm not certain I understand your meaning," the Ohioan said.

"Who can be wise, amazed, temperate and furious, loyal and neutral, in a moment? No man," Shakespeare quoted again, and chuckled.

Baxter glanced at Nate. "Does he go on like this often?"

"He has his spells."

"Do *you* understand him?"

"I don't try."

Shakespeare started stirring the contents of the tin with his butcher knife and sang out loudly, "Double, double toil and trouble; fire burn and cauldron bubble." He threw back his head and cackled uproariously.

"I'm glad I'm only staying a month," Baxter said, and moved off to be by himself.

Grinning, Nate sank down and observed the celestial display. He sympathized with poor Baxter; sometimes he was at a total loss to explain his friend's occasionally quirky behavior. Perhaps the reason for Shakespeare's bizarre sense of humor lay in the life the man had led, over four decades of living in the wild in the almost exclusive company of animals and Indians. Such an existence was bound to change a person.

A meteor streaked across the sky, leaving a glowing trail in its wake.

Nate's thoughts strayed to his wife, and he prayed she was faring well by herself. He'd been sorely tempted to bring her along, but Shakespeare had warned him they were venturing into Ute territory and had graphically detailed the bitter treatment she could expect from the Utes.

Far away a panther screamed.

Drowsiness assailed Nate, and he started to doze off once more. His eyes snapped open when he heard footsteps and smelled the delicious aroma of the stew.

"Here you are," Shakespeare said, squatting.

"I'm so hungry I could eat a bear," Nate joked, and smiled merrily.

The frontiersman shook his head, then slid his left arm under Nate's shoulders. "Let me help you sit up."

"I can manage."

"I'll help," Shakespeare said.

Nate allowed himself to be propped in a sitting position, and the tin was placed on his lap. Even through the blankets he felt the heat.

"Eat it slow," Shakespeare advised. "Chew on the bits of bear meat first, then sip of broth. If you eat too fast, you'll be sick." He offered his knife.

"I'll use my own," Nate stated, and pulled it out. He began eating slowly, convinced he'd never tasted such an exquisite meal.

"If you keep the stew down, you can have all you can eat for breakfast. By tomorrow afternoon I may even let you go for a walk."

Nate looked into the older man's kindly eyes. "I'll miss you when you go."

"Don't bring that up again."

"I can't help how I feel. Why, in many respects you're closer to me than my own father."

"You father never taught you the proper way to trap beaver."

"Don't mock me."

"I'm not. I'm simply pointing out that we've shared experiences your father never could, experiences that have drawn us close together in a special bond of friendship. You're being too hard on your father." Shakespeare paused, his brow creased, deep in contemplation. "It's not my habit to give advice unless someone asks, but in your case, since I care for you as if you were my own son, I'll make an exception."

Nate waited expectantly, astounded the mountain man would admit his affection.

"You should make the effort to go back to New York City one day," Shakespeare stated. "The ghosts of your past still haunt you, and the only way you'll put them to rest is by confronting them."

"I'll never go back there."

"All I ask is that you consider the idea."

"I will, but I'll never go back."

"Stubborn mule," Shakespeare muttered, and walked to the fire.

Shrugging, Nate bent to his meal, relishing every morsel. When he was done a pleasant warmth filled his belly and made him irresistibly sleepy. He deposited the tin pan at his side, reclined on his back, and within seconds drifted into a peaceful sleep.

Bright sunlight on his eyelids awakened him and he sat up to find the sun hovering above the eastern horizon and his companions gathering their equipment to go check the trap line. His head felt much better, and without thinking he tried to stand. Dizziness brought him down again, and he pressed his palm to his forehead and groaned.

"Stubborn, stubborn, stubborn," Shakespeare chided him. "I saw that. Stay put. I've already made coffee and several cakes, so you can relax and eat while we go freeze our feet."

"You used some of the flour?" Nate asked in surprise. Normally, the frontiersman reserved their meager supply for special occasions.

"I figured you need proper food, not just salty jerky."

"Thank you."

"I'll fetch your meal," Shakespeare said, and stepped closer.

"Let me do it," Nate objected. "I can't sit here the rest of my life. The sooner I get on my feet, the better. I promise I'll go slow."

"All right, but if you don't you'll be sorry." Shakespeare wedged a hatchet under his belt, hefted his rifle, and headed eastward.

"Take care of yourself, brother," Baxter said, and hiked after the frontiersman.

Nate watched them until they were lost from view. He glanced around the clearing and suddenly felt very alone, keenly aware of being a solitary human in the midst of a sea of often savage wildlife. To dispel the feeling he shook his head lightly and slowly pushed to his feet. The dizziness renewed its onslaught, but the attack wasn't as severe. He stood still until his sense of balance was restored, then stepped to the fire.

The fragrant aroma of the coffee tantalized his nostrils, and he hurriedly poured a cup and sat haunched near the flames. Between the fire and the coffee he was warm and comfortable in no time, and consuming a couple of tasty cakes further contributed to his peace of mind.

Nate listened to the wind in the trees and the songs of various birds. He saw a large specimen with a black head and blue plumage alight in a tree to the south and eye him warily for several minutes before flying boldly into the camp and landing on the opposite side of the campfire. Such birds were quite common at higher elevations, and the trappers referred to them as mountain jays. Unlike their noisy blue cousins in the East, these jays were remarkably reticent. "Hello, bird," he said to it, grateful for the company.

The jay hopped a few feet and tilted its head to inspect him from head to toe.

Impressed by the bird's audacity, Nate tossed crumbs to the ground, and grinned as the jay greedily devoured the bits. If only all the creatures in the Rockies were so friendly! he mused, and kept feeding his visitor until all the crumbs were gone. "That's all I have for now," he said.

Digesting the information in regal silence, the jay flapped its wings and soared off over the trees.

Chuckling, Nate poured more coffee and settled down to sip to his heart's content. Such tranquil moments were rare in the life of a mountaineer, and he intended to enjoy the interlude to the fullest.

Chipmunks scampered on boulders to the north, a rabbit hopped into sight near the spring, and a pair of ravens flew past overhead.

Nate contrasted the idyllic setting with the bear attack, and marveled at the wildly different faces Nature presented. One moment serene and beautiful, the next violent and ugly, Nature's temperament seemed to change with the breeze. If Nature possessed a personality, she would be labeled as fickle. Not to mention dangerous.

He touched his head, feeling the scalp, and found no bumps or scratches. Only then did he fully appreciate the magnitude of his fortune. A cut shoulder blade and a nicked foot were nothing compared to the alternative. To escape relatively unscathed from an encounter with a grizzly was rare enough; to do so several times constituted uncommon good luck.

The great Grizzly Killer!

Nate laughed at the thought and swallowed more perfectly sweetened coffee. If only his family could see him now! They'd probably laugh themselves to death. All except his father, who would criticize him for being a consummate fool.

He recalled Shakespeare's advice about returning to settle affairs, and he toyed with the notion of doing so. But if he did travel to the States, what about Winona? Dared he take her along? She might be overwhelmed by the experience and upset beyond measure. To someone attuned to the ways of the wilderness, the ways of the white race would border on madness. He decided to consider the matter at length later.

A horse whinnied loudly.

Nate glanced at the animals, contentedly grazing north of the spring, near the woods, and took another sip. If he felt up to the task later, he'd brush the mare and spend some time in her company. In a certain respect horses were a lot like people. If neglected, they tended to become moody. His mare was a headstrong animal prone to act up if not ridden or curried daily.

The same horse whinnied once more.

Belatedly, the coffee cup pressed to his lips, Nate realized the sound came from the southwest, not from the five animals near the spring. Alarmed, he shifted and stared into the forest.

Nothing moved.

He lowered the tin cup and straightened. Perhaps he'd been mistaken, he reasoned. Noises often echoed uncannily in the mountains. Perhaps one of their own horses had whinnied and the trees had reflected the sound from a different direction.

A flicker of motion proved otherwise.

Nate crouched and moved to his blankets. He

retrieved the Hawken, slanted to the right, and hurried behind a wide maple. The exertion produced a slight nausea, forcing him to rest his forehead on the trunk for a few seconds until the queasy sensation subsided, and when he did look to the southwest again the blood in his veins seemed to run cold as he laid eyes on an approaching Indian armed with a bow and arrows.

Chapter Six

The husky warrior had his eyes on the ground, scouring for tracks, and didn't see the camp until he casually gazed straight ahead and spotted the fire and the horses. He promptly reined up and sat still, watching intently.

Breathing shallowly, Nate froze and studied the Indian, trying to identify the man's tribe. He wasn't as skilled as Shakespeare; he couldn't tell at a glance if an Indian was a Sioux, Shoshone, Crow, Kiowa, or whatever.

Black hair hung well past the warrior's shoulders. Buckskin leggings and moccasins covered him from the waist down, but otherwise he was naked. In his right hand was the bow. A full quiver hung on his back, and a slender knife adorned his right hip.

Should he fire or not? Nate debated. If the man was hostile, then prudence dictated slaying him immediately. But what if the warrior was from a friendly tribe? As remote as the possibility might be, he couldn't afford to slay an innocent man. He opted to wait and observe what happened.

The Indian didn't budge for the longest while. At last he slid to the ground and advanced using every tree, bush, and thicket for cover, affording only fleeting glimpses of his darting form.

Nate drew his head back, squatted, and braced his left shoulder on the tree. He couldn't risk being spotted. In his condition he'd be no match for the warrior. As much as it tried his patience, he must wait, give the Indian time to enter the clearing, then spring a little surprise. If the warrior resisted, then he'd slay the man without compunction.

He held the rifle upright, his finger on the trigger, his thumb on the hammer, and slowly counted to fifty, anxious to take a peek. The seconds seemed like years. At last he inched his right eye to the edge of the trunk.

The warrior was in plain sight, an arrow nocked to his bow, standing at the south edge of the clearing with his head swinging from side to side. Apparently convinced the camp was temporarily unattended, he hurried to the fire and knelt next to the stacked packs containing the supplies. He glanced at the horses, then at the spring, then placed his bow on the grass and started to unfasten the top of a pack.

Nate had a perfect shot, but he couldn't bring himself to shoot. The Indian was in profile, intent on undoing the leather ties. He slowly stood, leveled the Hawken, and stepped boldly from concealment.

So engrossed was the warrior in discovering the contents of the pack, he didn't notice.

Well aware of how quickly an Indian could lift a bow and fire, Nate advanced several strides and deliberately cocked the hammer. The click had the desired effect.

Spinning, the Indian released the pack and grabbed for his bow, his eyes widening in consternation at being taken off guard.

"Don't!" Nate barked, aiming at the man's forehead.

His fingers about to close on the handle, the warrior stared at the unwavering Hawken and froze, his consternation changing to an expression of arrogant resentment.

"Take your hand off the bow," Nate said, and when the Indian showed no sign of complying he motioned with his head. "Step back, away from your weapon."

Even if the warrior didn't understand English, the motion and the tone were unmistakable. Reluctantly, he slid backwards and stood, his arms at his sides.

"Do you speak the white man's tongue?" Nate asked.

A stony silence was his response.

Nate walked to within three yards of the Indian. He wagged the Hawken at the man's knife and pointed at the ground.

Scowling, the warrior used two fingers to pull the knife from its sheath and dropped it. He exhaled loudly and awaited further instructions.

"Move back away from the packs," Nate said, and gestured with the rifle to get his point across. When the Indian obeyed, he motioned for the man to sit. "I'll bet you're a murdering Blackfoot."

The warrior said nothing.

Nate began to relax. There was no way the man could jump him before he fired, and the Indian knew it. He cradled the rifle in the crook of his right arm and addressed the prisoner in sign language, his fingers flying. Shakespeare and Winona had spent many hours instructing him in the universal language of the tribes, and he'd become quite proficient. "Are you a Blackfoot?"

Jutting his chin out defiantly, the Indian refused to answer.

"You act like a Blackfoot," Nate said, knowing a member of any other tribe would be insulted by the comment. He almost grinned when it elicited a response.

"The Blackfeet are cowardly dogs. They deserve to be rubbed out of existence."

"Are you a Crow?"

The warrior snorted contemptuously. "You are very ignorant, white man. I am better than any Crow. They are bigger cowards than the Blackfeet and flee at the mention of my tribe."

"What is your tribe?"

Squaring his broad shoulders, the man stated proudly, "The Utes."

Nate nodded. Since they were trapping in Ute territory, the man must be speaking the truth. "I know the Utes well. They are brave fighters."

Surprise registered at the unexpected compliment. "How do you know about my people?" the warrior asked.

"I have fought them a couple of times."

"And you are still alive?"

Grinning, Nate moved a few feet to his right to put the fire between them. "I have fought the Blackfeet too, and I can tell you they are not cowards."

The warrior wasn't interested in the Blackfeet. "How many of my people have you killed?"

Nate had to think for a moment. "Thirteen, I believe."

A crimson tinge of anger flushed the Ute's cheeks and he clenched his fists for a full five seconds before responding. "You lie. No white man has ever killed so many Utes."

"I have," Nate signed calmly.

The warrior's eyes narrowed and he scrutinized the young mountain man from head to toe. "How are you known?"

"There are no signs for my white name. Some time ago I earned an Indian name, though, and many now call me by it."

"What is this name?"

"Grizzly Killer."

The Ute's eyes strayed to the rack of drying bear meat. His brow creased and he seemed to be deep in thought. "During the Thunder Moon a warrior named Buffalo Horn led a war party of thirteen men from my village. They never came back."

"I killed twelve of them. Another time I killed one other warrior. All of them were trying to slay me when they died," Nate reflected.

Disbelief wrestled with acceptance on the Ute's countenance, and finally the truth prevailed. Strangely, he smiled. "I will be honored to take your scalp one day."

"Many have tried."

"For one so young to have counted so many coup, you must be a brave warrior."

"I did what I did to survive, nothing more."

"You survive quite well."

Nate smiled. "What is your name?"

"I am Two Owls."

"Did you come here looking for us?"

"No," the Ute replied. "I was hunting when I came across horse tracks and followed them until I saw your fire."

Baxter's tracks, Nate reflected. "Did you see any sign of the Blackfeet war party?"

Two Owls stiffened. "What war party?"

"The prints you followed were made by a companion of mine who was escaping from a band of Blackfeet."

Tremendously upset by the news, the Ute began to rise, then caught himself. His hands and arms moved emphatically. "The Blackfeet can be in this area for only one reason. They are planning to raid my village.

You must let me go warn my people."

Taken unawares by the request, Nate hesitated before answering. Although he agreed with the Ute's conclusion, and even though he sympathized with the warrior's fears for the village, he wasn't about to release a member of a tribe devoted to the extermination of all trappers. "I am sorry. I cannot."

Two Owl's featured clouded. When he signed, he stabbed the air. "I should have known better than to ask a white."

"I will talk it over with my friends when they return. If they agree, we will let you go."

"When will they return?"

"I do not know."

The Ute sullenly accepted the inevitable, but he cast a longing glance at the horses.

"Do you have a wife?" Nate asked.

"A wife and three sons," the warrior replied proudly. "My boys will grow up to become great fighters and their names will be feared by all their enemies."

"Is your village near here?"

Two Owls lifted his hands to respond, then paused and grinned. "You are crafty like a coyote, Grizzly Killer."

"I am?"

"You almost tricked me into revealing the location of my people. This I will not do."

"We are not here to harm your tribe."

"Why are you in this region?"

"To trap beaver."

Frowning in displeasure, Two Owls nodded. "I guessed as much. Your kind will one day wipe the beaver out."

"You are being unfair. There are many thousands of beavers in the mountains and only a few hundred trappers. We will never wipe them out."

"I would expect you to say such things. You are

white. But my eyes are the eyes of a Ute, and I know what I know. Already have the whites killed more beaver in the past few winters than all the tribes have killed since the day the Great Mystery breathed life into all creatures."

Nate chuckled at the concept. "You have an excellent imagination."

"Laugh at me if you want, but my words are true. Why do you think my people dislike the whites so much? It is because we know the whites are destroyers and we do not want your kind to destroy the land that has fed us and clothed us for more generations than there are fingers to count with," Two Owls sighed solemnly.

"I do not know what I can say to change your mind, so I will only say you are wrong. Why would my people want the beaver to die off when they depend on the beaver for their existence?"

"My people have often discussed that very question, and we have decided the whites must all be crazy."

At this Nate laughed openly.

Two Owls regarded him reflectively for a while. "This is most odd," he stated at length.

"What is?"

"I find myself liking you."

"Have you ever talked with a white man before?"

"No."

"So this is a first for both of us. You are not the rabid killer I believed all Utes to be. You are a man, nothing more, nothing less, and perhaps that is the answer to all the questions both of us have. My people and your people live differently and have different values, but they are all still people. Instead of hating each other because of our differences, we should try to understand one another and live in peace."

The Ute appeared amazed. "I never expected to

hear such words from a white man."

Sighing, Nate indicated the surrounding mountains with a sweep of his right arm. "I have made my home here. I want to raise a family and watch my sons grow into manhood, just like you do. Naturally, I would rather live in peace with all the tribes."

"No one will ever live in peace with the Blackfeet."

"I know," Nate signed. "Fortunately, their villages are far to the north and they only travel to this region for occasional raids." He saw the Ute's lips compress, and realized he'd made a tactless mistake by reminding the warrior of the danger to the Ute village. Guilt troubled his conscience. How could he detain the warrior knowing the man's wife and children were in imminent danger? If only Shakespeare would get back! The mountain man would know what to do.

"Do I just sit here until your friends return?" Two Owls inquired.

"Yes."

"Then you will want to bind me."

"Not if you give me your word of honor that you will do as I say."

"You would trust *my* word?"

"Yes."

Two Owls leaned on his palms, his mouth pursed. Then he began to sign, "Grizzly Killer, you are unlike any white man I have ever heard of. If more whites were like you, my people would not hate them so much."

"When you are among your people again, tell them about this. Perhaps many will agree with you."

"I will tell them, but most will still dislike all trappers."

Nate was about to make a comment when the distant crack of a rifle turned his gaze to the east. His pulse quickened. As far as he knew, Shakespeare was the only other man within a radius of miles who had a rifle, and there was no logical reason for the mountain man to be using his Hawken to slay beaver.

Another shot sounded, not quite as loud, the distinct blast of a flintlock.

Was that Baxter? Nate took a stride eastward, dread gripping his soul, dread that intensified a moment later when, so faint he could barely hear them, there arose a series of blood-curdling war whoops.

Chapter Seven

Nate glanced at Two Owls and debated whether to simply release the warrior, wondering if the whoops were from Blackfeet or Utes. He must go find his friends, but it wouldn't be wise to force the warrior to accompany him since he couldn't effectively watch a prisoner and be alert for an ambush at the same time. A second shot from a flintlock decided the issue and he quickly signed, "You are free to go." Whirling, he grabbed his bridle from his pile of tack but didn't bother with the saddle, then sprinted toward the horses, moving as fast as he dared, still weak but determined not to buckle.

Another rifle discharged.

Please let them be alive! Nate prayed. He slowed as he neared the animals so he wouldn't spook them, and stepped to the mare to hastily remove her hobble. Sliding on the bridle took another moment. He swung onto her and hauled on the reins, breaking into a gallop immediately, and rode across the clearing, passing the fire enroute.

Two Owls was gone.

A brief dizziness assailed him as he plunged into the trees. Fortunately his head cleared and he could concentrate on avoiding low limbs and entangling thickets. The mare responded superbly, as she always did, her hooves pounding, dirt flying.

Nate covered fifty yards before he detected movement out of the corner of his right eye and glanced to the south to behold the Ute riding hard to catch up. The grin creasing the warrior's mouth served to confirm his intentions were friendly, and Nate allowed the man to draw alongside the mare. Together they raced on.

Anxiety distorted Nate's perception of time. It seemed as if only a few minutes elapsed between leaving the camp and arriving at the west bank of the stream, although the sweat lathering his skin and the mare testified to a longer duration. He halted and looked both ways.

Two Owls pointed northward and used sign language to say, "We must go that way."

Relying on the Indian's superior instincts, Nate turned and rode along the waterway, traveling two hundred yards before he spied several traps lying in the grass. Goading the mare forward, he practically vaulted from her back to crouch beside the three Newhouses. Under no circumstances whatsoever would Shakespeare or Baxter leave prized traps unattended. He scanned the forest on both sides of the stream and saw nothing out of the ordinary.

Two Owls climbed from his black stallion and bent over to inspect the ground. He grunted and his hands flew. "There has been a fight here. See how the grass is bent?" He touched a patch of crushed blades. "Many Indians and two whites fought."

"How do you know there were two whites?"

The Ute pointed at Nate's moccasins. "White men

do not walk as Indians do. Your kind carry too much of their weight on their heels and tread heavily. My people always walk lightly like the wolves and the big cats."

Nate looked at the ground, wishing he could read sign with such skill. "What else can you tell me?"

"The whites ran into the trees that way," Two Owls said, and nodded to the west.

Springing onto the mare, Nate rode off. If the Ute was right, then his friends must be hoping they could lose their pursuers in the woods and swing around to the camp. But was it Blackfeet or Utes doing the pursuing? If the latter, his temporary truce with Two Owls might well result in an arrow in the back.

The answer was discovered unexpectedly.

They had ridden for only a minute, always bearing due west, when the mare neighed and shied away from an object in her path.

Nate reined up and looked down to discover a buckskin-clad body sprawled in the weeds. Fearing the worst, he slid to the earth and stood over the corpse. Sweet relief brought an unconscious smile at recognizing the dead man was an Indian.

Dropping from the stallion, Two Owls knelt and rolled the man over. "A Blackfoot dog," he said.

A crimson-rimmed hole in the center of the warrior's forehead revealed the cause of death. A few inches from his left hand was a war club.

"We must be very careful," Two Owls advised. "The Blackfeet will return for this body."

"They must be close," Nate said, and remounted to lead the way, moving slower, his rifle across his thighs.

Not so much as a chipmunk chattered in the surrounding forest. The patterns of Nature had been disrupted, transforming the normally vibrant woodland into a silent expanse of motionless vegetation.

Where were his friends? Nate chided himself for not insisting on accompanying them. If they were dead, his guilt would be boundless. He spied a hill not far off, and scrutinized its tree-covered slope to no avail.

Two Owls fell behind a few yards.

Nate decided to go over the hill instead of skirting it. Once on top he'd have an unobstructed view of the countryside and might spot the frontiersman and the Ohioan. With that in mind he urged the mare up the gradual slope, following a game trail, and he was almost to the crest when he heard the alien sound.

Laughter.

Harsh, gloating laughter.

Jerking on the reins, Nate took the mare into a dense stand of saplings and halted. The Ute joined him.

Slowly the laughter and chuckles grew louder. Distinct voices could be heard, talking excitedly.

The language was unfamiliar to Nate, and he deduced it must be the Blackfoot tongue. Twisting, he gazed toward the top, and shortly thereafter six warriors appeared, all in good spirits as if intoxicated by the flush of victory. They made their way down the hill and to the east, apparently going to retrieve the body of their comrade.

Nate watched them in horror. If the Blackfeet were so happy, there could only be one reason. Shakespeare and Baxter must be dead. He suddenly felt weak again and sagged, holding onto the pommel for support. Dazed by the magnitude of the calamity, unable to formulate a plan of action, he sat there until Two Owls poked him in the arm. With an effort he turned.

"What is wrong with you?" the warrior inquired.

"My friends . . . " Nate began, and his hands slumped.

"Your friends are probably still alive."

"What makes you think so?"

"The Blackfeet love to torture even more than they love to kill and steal, and they are very fond of tormenting whites. They might have taken your friends alive."

Nate had raised his arms to express his pessimism when more conversation came from the other side of the hill. Tensing, he riveted his eyes on the crest until additional Blackfeet showed up and counted them as they came over. Two. Four. Five. A few seconds went by, and then the sixth person walked into view and Nate wanted to shout for joy.

Shakespeare had his arms bound behind his back. His hat was gone, his hair tousled, his weapons missing. He stepped proudly, his chin jutting defiantly.

After the mountain man came Thaddeus Baxter. His arms were also tied, his flintlock was gone, and a nasty gash marked his left cheek. His strides were unsteady and he blinked a lot.

Nate rashly gripped the reins firmly to charge for cover, his emotions getting the better of his reason, but he was jolted back to reality by the appearance of even more Blackfeet.

Three sturdy warriors brought up the rear, two armed with bows, the third with a fusee. They were clearly ready to fire if the captives made a bid to escape.

Reluctantly, Nate let them all pass. The odds were simply too great, 14 to one in favor of the Blackfeet. Fourteen to two if he counted Two Owls on his side. When the party disappeared in the forest below, he glanced at his newfound companion. "What will the Blackfeet do next?"

The Ute answered with the certainty of one who knew his lifelong enemies well. "They will bury their dead. By tomorrow they will be on their way back to their village where your friends will be put to death."

"How long will it take them to reach their village?"

"Perhaps twelve suns. Less if they travel fast."

The information gave Nate an idea. Apparently Shakespeare and Baxter were safe enough for the time being, at least until they reached the village. His wisest recourse was to shadow the war party and wait for an opportunity to effect a rescue. Twelve days was a long time. A lot could happen.

"What will you do?" Two Owls asked.

"I will follow the Blackfeet and free my friends."

"Alone?"

"If I must."

The reply caused the Ute to straighten. "This is not my fight."

"I know."

"I have a family waiting for me."

"I know."

"I cannot help you, Grizzly Killer," Two Owls said, and frowned. "I truly wish I could."

Although his hopes were dashed, Nate kept his face impassive and shrugged. "I understand."

"You are not angry?"

"Why should I be? You have been honest with me. They are my friends; I must save them."

Two Owls stared into Nate's eyes, then wheeled his horse and looked back. "I go now. I will tell my people what has happened and try to convince them to send a war party to stop the Blackfeet, but I do not know if they will come if it means helping whites."

"I can ask no more," Nate signed.

"May the Great Mystery guide your footsteps."

"And yours."

A curt nod and a wave and the Ute was gone.

The enormity of the mountains seemed to weigh down on Nate's shoulders and shook his head to dispel a gloomy premonition of disaster. He was alone. So be it. But he could accomplish what had to be done if he stayed alert and exercised single-minded determination.

He rode slowly down the hill and dismounted at its base. Taking hold of the reins he hiked eastward, proceeding with the utmost caution, until he spotted the war party. Two of the warriors were carrying their deceased fellow warrior as the band walked toward the stream. Keeping well back, Nate trailed them, stopping when they halted on the west bank of the stream.

The Blackfeet compelled Shakespeare and Baxter to sit, deposited the body near them, and set to work making a camp.

Were they planning to stay the night right there? Nate wondered. If so, it would give him time to return to the camp, load the pack animals, and return before daylight. He watched from concealment as they used their tomahawks to chop off and strip long, straight limbs that were arranged in a conical shape much like their buffalo-hide lodges. Three of these improvised forts were constructed, and when they were completed Shakespeare and the Ohioan were rudely shoved into the middle fort and two guards were posted.

A tall, lean warrior evidently was in charge. He had issued instructions to the others during the building of the forts, and now he dispatched four of his tribesmen to the north, possibly to do some hunting. His frame and his mien set him apart, as did one other factor. In addition to a bow and arrows, he carried an extraordinary weapon tucked under a slender leather cord looped about his slim waist: a gleaming sword.

Nate was too far away to note the shape of the hilt, but from the general outline he surmised the sword must be Spanish. He couldn't begin to imagine how the Blackfoot had come to possess it, unless a war party had once conducted a raid down toward Santa Fe, which was highly unlikely because of the vast distance involved. Another possibility occurred to him. Many years ago the Spanish had mined much gold of the central Rockies. If the Blackfeet had attacked a gold train or mining camp, the sword could have been taken from a halpless conquistador and bequeathed from father to son, generation to generation.

Once satisfied the Blackfeet truly intended to remain at their camp for quite some time, Nate stealthily moved to the southwest, mounted when the forts were out of sight, and headed off at a gallop.

He realized the lives of two brave men were in his hands, and formulated various plans for saving them, everything from picking the Blackfeet off one by one to setting their forts on fire in the middle of the night. No matter how he looked at the problem, there was no way to liberate Shakespeare and Baxter without running the risk of losing their lives.

Nate's stomach reminded him he needed nourishment if he was to replenish the vitality he'd lost due to his injuries. His convalescence had been cut short just when he needed to be at the peak of his strength, and a grueling journey to Blackfoot territory promised to aggravate his condition.

He stopped twice to orient himself, and had begun to doubt he'd traveled in the right direction when he spied a wisp of smoke curling above the treetops. Thank goodness the camp was far enough from the Blackfeet so they hadn't noticed it!

Nate relaxed and slowed the mare to a walk. There was no sense in overexerting her until the need arose.

He estimated a half hour would be required to load all the pack animals and string the horses in a line. In an hour or so he could be back there watching over his friends.

He thought about Two Owls, and speculated on whether the Utes would help. Given their long-standing hatred of trappers, he doubted they would lift a finger.

Soon the clearing was visible, the campfire dying down, the horses standing near the spring, the packs undisturbed.

Nate rode into the camp and hopped down. No sooner did his moccasins touch the ground then a savage shriek shattered the stillness to his rear, and pivoting he saw a mounted Indian bearing down on him with an upraised lance poised to throw.

Chapter Eight

Nate instinctively raised the Hawken to fire, but in a flash of insight he realized the sound of the shot would carry to the Blackfeet and might lead them to his location. Instead of squeezing the trigger he darted to the right and dived for the ground. In his ears drummed the pounding hooves of the warrior's mount, and a second later something brushed his right shoulder and thudded into the earth at his side.

A tremendous whoop issued from bloodthirsty lips as the Indian bore down on him.

Rolling to the left, Nate tried to push erect. A heavy body slammed onto his back, stunning him, driving him down again, and he lost his grip on the rifle. Knees gouged him in the spine and strong hands looped around his chin from behind. He dimly realized the man was trying to break his neck, and frantically flipped onto his right side while at the same instant he whipped his left elbow back and around.

The warrior grunted and was sent flying.

Nate scrambled to his knees, struggling to clear

his thoughts, keenly aware he must prevail or perish. Twisting, he saw the Indian springing at his chest, and managed to jerk aside at the last moment.

Exceptionally agile, the warrior came down on his hands and knees and almost in the same motion jumped erect, drawing a tomahawk before he straightened.

Pushing to his feet, Nate saw his attacker's face clearly for the first time, and was shocked by the unbridled hatred displayed. The tomahawk arced at his head and he skipped to the left, his hands dropping to his pistols. Again he changed his mind. He must slay the warrior quietly, and the only way to do so was by using his butcher knife. With the thought his knife leaped from its sheath.

Hissing in fury, the Indian swung the tomahawk several times in succession, relying on his weapon's greater reach.

Forced to retreat, Nate dodged the swipes and countered with his knife, striving to slash his foe's abdomen or chest. The warrior deftly deflected the blade every time, increasing the temptation to employ the pistols. Try as he might Nate couldn't break through the other's defenses. To compound his predicament, his arms grew steadily more fatigued. If he wanted to survive he must do something and do it quickly.

An idea struck heartbeats later. Since he had the shorter weapon and couldn't hope to stab the Indian in the torso, why not take advantage of the knife's lighter weight and ease of handling?

Enraged by his failure to kill, the Indian swung wildly.

Nate backpedaled further, biding his time, and when the warrior overextended a swing and exposed the arm holding the tomahawk, he was ready. The knife flicked straight out and speared into the Indian's wrist, cutting deep and causing blood to gush forth.

If Nate expected the wound would prompt the Indian to surrender or flee, he was sadly mistaken. To his surprise the warrior shifted the tomahawk to the other hand and renewed the assault more furiously than before.

Now the fight became a desperate battle of endurance. Would the Indian weaken first from the loss of so much blood or would Nate collapse from the strain to his system?

Nate sensed he couldn't hold out much longer, and gambled everything on a last-ditch effort. He deliberately let his adversary get a little closer, let the tomahawk miss his stomach by a hair, and lunged forward to plunge his knife to the hilt below the warrior's sternum.

Gasping, the Indian stiffened, staggered, and clutched at Nate's wrist. Eyes widening, the warrior attempted to raise the tomahawk for a final blow, but his limbs betrayed him. He groaned as his legs began to buckle.

With a sharp tug Nate tore the knife free and stepped back to watch the Indian sink to the grass. The man rested on his knees, his hands going limp, and released the tomahawk. Nate kicked the weapon out of reach.

Defiant eyes were turned to the youth and a string of words were barked in an unknown tongue.

"You must be a Blackfoot," Nate signed wearily.

Not a sound came from the warrior, who doubled over and pressed both hands to his midriff.

Nate wanted to put the man out of his misery, and considered plunging the knife in again. But he needed answers, and the only one who could supply them was rapidly dying. He nudged the Indian with his left foot.

Up snapped the warrior's chin, his lips curled in a snarl.

"Who are you?" Nate signed, holding the hilt of the bloody knife with just the last two fingers on his right hand. "Why did you try to kill me?"

Gritting his teeth, the Indian moved his arms awkwardly. "White dog! You have more luck than ten ordinary men."

"Who are you? What tribe are you from?"

The warrior answered with difficulty, his fingers fluttering unsteadily. "I am proud to be a Blackfoot. One day we will kill all white dogs."

"Are you part of the war party I saw a while ago?"

"You saw my brothers. I am part of White Bear's band." The Blackfoot paused, breathing raggedly, and signed his spite. "I pray the maggots eat your intestines before another moon passes. May the vultures feast on your rotten heart and the worms on your flesh. You are—" he began to sign, and gagged, his mouth slackening. His eyelids quivered, his tongue protruded, and he pitched onto his face.

For the longest time Nate simply stood there, staring at his vanquished foe. Such hatred! He'd never known anyone to express such sheer malice. The Blackfoot had cursed him with his dying breath. And why? Just because of the color of his skin.

What had the man meant about his brothers? Was the remark meant literally, or in the sense that all men in a tribe were considered to be spiritual brothers? He realized the man had not bothered to give his name, but at least he now knew the name of the tall Indian with the sword. White Bear.

A low whinny brought Nate out of his reflection to stare at the Blackfoot's horse. It wore a leather bridle, not the rope war bridle usually used by Indians on a raid. He remembered Baxter telling how his pack animal was stolen, and deduced this must be the same animal. But why was a lone Blackfoot riding it so far from the rest of the band? Had this man been sent to scout for the Ute village and found the camp instead, then decided to wait and ambush whoever showed up?

Feeling extremely fatigued, Nate stepped to the fading fire and sat down to rest. He could afford five minutes, no more. And more than anything else he needed food. He wiped the knife clean on the grass, slid the blade back into the sheath, and walked to the rack of drying grizzly meat. Most of the strips would have to be left behind. What a waste. He grabbed a handful and returned to the fire to eat.

What was he going to do about the horses? Not counting his mare, there were five animals to lead. Would he jeopardize his chances to rescuing Shakespeare and Baxter if he took all of them along? They were bound to make noise. But if he stayed far enough from the war party the odds of being heard or seen were quite slim. Since horses were one of a man's most valuable commodities in the wild, along with a good rifle, he elected to take them.

The bear meat tasted tangy and made him thirsty. After eating he ventured to the spring and drank his fill, gulping the cold water and letting it spill over his lips and chin. With his meal out of the way, he prepared for the pursuit.

First he buried the Blackfoot. Not that he felt any obligation to treat the warrior in a civilized manner, but he didn't want any buzzards to circle overhead and draw attention to the campsite.

Next he loaded the supplies onto the horses, distributing the packs evenly on his pack animal, Shakespeare's pack animal, Baxter's pack animal, and Baxter's horse. This way the horses carried lighter loads and could move faster. He didn't put any packs on the mountain man's white horse. Like the mare, it was one of the family, so to speak, and deserved better treatment.

He crammed as much bear meat into several packs

as he could, knowing the opportunities to hunt on the trail would be few and far between. Then he extinguished the fire and scattered the ashes with his foot. The horses were permitted to slake their thirst, and in short order he was mounted and leading the string in the direction of the Blackfoot forts.

Was there anything he'd forgotten? Both pistols were loaded and wedged under his belt and the Hawken was across his thighs. He'd tossed the warrior's lance into the trees, but kept the tomahawk; it now nestled in a pack beside a different tomahawk he'd taken from another Blackfoot months ago.

All the way back he worried the Blackfeet would be gone. He grinned when he drew close enough to see the forts and saw several warriors moving about. They were three hundred yards off, which was as close as he dared get.

Nate dismounted, hid the horses in a dense stand of pines, and moved a dozen yards nearer to spy on the war party. He hoped to catch a glimpse of his friends. The guards were still posted outside the middle fort, but Shakespeare and Baxter never appeared.

The remaining hours of the day dragged past. Nate refused to leave again, no matter what, and occupied himself noting the activities of the Blackfeet. The quartet dispatched earlier returned bearing a dead deer. Two others spent their time fishing. Others gathered roots. Despite being in Ute territory, they posted no sentries.

Evening arrived. The Blackfeet entered their forts and shortly thereafter smoke poured from the tops of each. The many tales he'd heard about the fierce warriors of the northern plains and mountains were all true, as he well knew from prior experience. They were a proud people, the toughest tribe on the

frontier, the most feared of all, and they were aware
of the fact. They adopted a condescending attitude
toward other tribes and would never show fear, even
in the face of overwhelming odds.

Night settled in. Nate went to his pack animal and
took a blanket from a pack. Covering his shoulders,
he stepped to his vantage point and continued
watching.

Except for emerging to relieve themselves or to
enjoy some fresh air, the Blackfeet stayed in their
forts. Loud laughter intermittently wafted on the
breeze. Once, incredibly, the occupants of the
northernmost fort burst into song, a rhythmic chant
that went on for half an hour.

Nate ate more cold bear meat before retiring. He
curled up at the base of a tree, pulled the blanket
tight, and closed his eyes, wishing he had a cozy fire
to lie beside. In his mind's eye he reviewed the day's
events and counted himself fortunate to be alive. If
he wanted to stay that way, tomorrow he would have
to be more alert, more cautious, than ever before. One
mistake could cost him his life, not to mention the
consequences for the mountain man and the Ohioan.
He hoped he wouldn't have any difficulty in falling
asleep, and didn't.

The chattering of a squirrel in the tree above
awoke Nate with a start and he sat up, blinking and
trying to organize his thoughts. He glanced at the sun
and thought he must be dreaming. It hung well
above the eastern horizon. The morning was half
over.

Shakespeare and Baxter!

He leaped upright and stared at the forts. There
wasn't a Blackfoot anywhere. No! No! No! He
couldn't have slept so long. Stumbling in his haste,
he ran to the horses, untied them, put the blanket

in a pack, and mounted the mare. Of all the times to oversleep! Why now? Why when Shakespeare needed him the most?

Nate galloped to the forts and didn't bother to inspect them. There was no doubt the war party had departed hours ago, probably at first light. But which way? He looked in all directions and finally chose to go north. Their home territory was to the north. Hopefully, they would also stick with the stream for as far as they could.

Kneeing the mare, he gave belated chase. Since the warriors were on foot, they would leave few tracks, certainly not enough for an inexperienced tracker to follow. He kept his gaze on the land ahead, praying he would spot them before they saw him.

He traveled a mile. Two. Three. Still there was no sign of the band. Stubbornly he pressed on, refusing to give up. If, as he surmised, the war party had headed out at daylight, and if they covered four miles an hour, which was about the average over such rugged terrain, and if the current time was between nine and ten, then the Blackfeet had already gone twelve miles. Nine or ten more and he would be close on their heels.

Nate ignored everything around him. All he cared about was catching up. When the pack horses lagged he tugged brutally on the rope. He tried not to think about what would happen if he failed to find the band. If they had turned from the stream at any point, his companions were doomed.

Four more miles went by. Once he spooked a small herd of mountain buffalo, and another time a panther bounded into the underbrush at his approach.

The higher the sun climbed, the hotter it became. Sweat caked his skin, and he repeatedly moped his sleeve across his forehead. By all rights he should stop and let the animals drink, but he refused. They would drink when he did.

When he'd gone over ten miles he slowed slightly, afraid he would blunder upon the war party and ruin everything. Two more miles fell behind him and still they didn't appear. He saw a bend in the stream two hundred yards to the north, a gradual loop to the west. Trees prevented him from seeing beyond it. Slowing even more, he warily neared the bend, riding along a narrow strip of clear ground at the water's edge. With his attention exclusively focused on the curve, he neglected to scan the trees at his left elbow, and paid for his oversight when a muscular form hurtled from a limb and slammed him from the saddle.

Chapter Nine

Nate came down hard on his back, the Indian straddling him, and felt a hand clamped over his mouth. He looked up, expecting to see a knife or tomahawk spearing at his chest, and instead saw the smiling face of Two Owls. Astounded, he simply lay there as the Ute slid off and signed a greeting.

"We meet again, Grizzly Killer."

In order to communicate Nate had to push himself into a sitting posture. "What are you doing here?" he bluntly asked.

"Repaying the debt I owe you."

"What debt?" Nate inquired in confusion.

"You spared me, gave me my freedom. My life was in your hands, yet you chose not to take it. More importantly, you treated me as a human being, with respect and dignity. Now I am here to repay the debt."

Nate was about to inform the Ute it wasn't necessary when he remembered the overriding sense of obligation and duty Indians possessed. If you did

Indians a kindness they naturally expected to be able to return the favor, and were insulted if you refused.

Two Owls pointed at the bend. "If I had not stopped you, you would have ridden straight into the war party. They are resting up ahead."

"Thank you," Nate said, wondering why the warrior didn't just voice a warning.

As if he'd sensed Nate's thoughts, Two Owls related, "I would have called out to you but you do not speak the Ute tongue. And also, I did not want to be shot if you mistook me for a Blackfoot."

Nate looked around. "Did any of your people come with you?"

"No."

"Why not?"

"It was as I told you it would be. I explained all that had happened to me and advised them you are a man to be trusted, a man deserving of our help, and although some of there were of the same opinion, the majority refused to aid a white man."

"But what about the Blackfeet? Surely they wanted to send warriors to repulse the invaders."

"Some did. The others were of the opinion our tribe should devote itself to protecting the village, which at this very moment they are in the process of moving far to the south."

"They are running?"

Two Owls's lips tightened. "There are scores of women, children, and the elderly in our village. Would you have us leave all of them unprotected while the warriors go after the Blackfeet?"

"But there are only fourteen. Your tribe can easily defeat them."

"Where there are fourteen there are often fifty. The Blackfeet frequently divide their war parties into smaller bands and spread out to cover more area. My people could not be certain there is just this one small band."

"So you came back all by yourself," Nate signed, and only then fully appreciated the implications. Here was a Ute warrior, sworn enemy of all trappers and mountain men, hazarding his life to assist a white man. And why? Not because of an abiding bond of friendship; they'd hardly known each other. No, it was beause of the basic bond of shared humanity.

Two Owls grinned. "The Blackfeet should not be allowed to raid our country with impunity."

"How did your family feel about your leaving?"

"My wife was not happy but she did not object. My sons were excited and asked me to bring home the hair of many Blackfeet."

Standing, Nate brushed twigs and dirt from his buckskins and reclaimed his rifle. "Did you see my friends?"

"Yes. They are still alive. I returned to the Blackfoot camp shortly before sunrise and watched them leave, then followed. I am very surprised you did not appear. Where were you?"

Nate wasn't about to embarrass himself by disclosing he'd overslept, so he fibbed. "I was jumped by a lone Blackfoot at my camp and killed him." Before he could begin a lengthy elaboration the Ute interrupted.

"What did you do with him?"

"Buried the body. What else?"

Two Owls looked at the pack animals. "Where is his hair?"

"I let him keep it."

The warrior looked bewildered. "You did not scalp him?"

"I forgot."

Two Owls shook his head several times. "I will never understand the white man if I live a hundred and twenty winters."

For want of anything better to say, Nate signed, "One hundred and twenty winters? No one lives that long."

"Many of our people do. And I have heard of men from other tribes who lived equally as long."

One hundred and twenty years? Nate decided to check into the matter later. Right now he walked to the mare and patted her neck, thankful she hadn't spooked when the Ute jumped him.

Two Owls came over. "Do you want to see the Blackfoot camp?"

"Yes."

"Come with me."

Obediently Nate trailed after the warrior as Two Owls angled into the trees and headed northward. They crept forward until they could see the stream again. Seated or lying at ease on the bank, approximately 75 yards from the curve, were the Blackfeet. Positioned on their knees near the water, probably so they couldn't try to flee into the woods, were Shakespeare and Baxter. The Ohioan sagged, the worse for wear, but the mountain man had his shoulders squared and his eyes fixed balefully on his captors.

"They will leave soon," Two Owls disclosed. "We must be ready to follow."

Nate let the warrior lead them back to his horses. On the way Two Owls detoured a few dozen yards and retrieved his own horse.

Once back in the saddle, Nate rode slowly toward the bend. The Ute came alongside.

"Tonight I will begin to pick them off."

"What do you mean?"

Two Owls reached back and patted the bow slung in its buckskin case over his left shoulder. "I will kill them one by one."

"Is that wise?"

"We are outnumbered. We must reduce the odds."

"And the Blackfeet will know we are after them."

"So? They have a great deal distance to travel. In five suns most of them will be dead."

"And what am I supposed to do while you are picking them off?"

"Stay far back. They will not find you."

Nate reined up and the Ute did the same. "What about my friends? What will the Blackfeet do to them?"

Two Owls shrugged. "I do not know."

"The Blackfeet might kill them."

"Perhaps. But I doubt it. The Blackfeet want to take them back to their village."

"Once you start killing those warriors, who knows what will happen? I am sorry. I cannot permit you to kill any Blackfeet until I have freed my friends."

"You can not *permit* me?" Two Owls said.

"No."

"How will you stop me?"

"I will do whatever is necessary," Nate stated, leaving the rest to the Ute's imagination. He detected a flicker of resentment in the warrior's eyes and tensed. This would be a true test of how much he could rely on the man.

A minute elapsed during which Two Owls stared at the youth without blinking. Finally he nodded curtly. "As you wish. I will not slay the dogs until you have rescued your friends."

"Thank you again."

"Provided you can free them within two days," Two Owl added.

Nate frowned. Why the time constraint? What difference did it make if he took two days or ten? "Two days is not enough time."

"It is all I can spare. In three days they will be at the limit of Ute territory and I promised my wife I would go no further. Giving you two days leaves me one day to kill as many of them as I can."

"And if I do not agree?"

"In three days I start killing whether you have rescued your companions or not."

There was no doubt the Ute meant it. Nate had two choices. Push the issue and possibly have a fight on his hands or cause Two Owls to go off and stalk the war party now, or play along and try to save Shakespeare and Baxter in the alloted time. Since forty-eight hours were better than none, he chose to agree. "I will try to save them within two days."

"Good. Do not fear. Two days is more than enough."

"I hope so."

They rode to within ten feet of the bend and dismounted to check on the band. The Blackfeet were already on the march, staying close to the stream, the captives walking at the middle of the ragged line.

Nate waited until the war party was out of sight, then climbed on the mare and headed out. He went slowly, well aware a single mistake could prove fatal. Although he resented the time limitation imposed by the Ute, secretly he was glad for the warrior's company. No one knew how to fight Indians better than another Indian, and the Ute's advice could prove invaluable.

Two Owls paced his stallion to the left of the mare. "Do you mind if we talk?" he asked.

"What about?"

"I am very curious to learn about the ways of the white man. We have heard many strange stories, some of which can not possibly be true."

"What kind of stories?" Nate responded.

"My people have been told the whites believe they can own land, can buy and sell it just as they would a horse or a dog. Is this true?"

"Yes."

Two Owls chuckled. "This is foolish. The land

belongs to all. No one person has any right to own even a blade of grass. The land is ours to roam over as we please." He paused. "Is it also true the whites live in great stone villages where in the winter the air is choked with smoke from their fires?"

"This is also true."

"And most whites in these stone villages do not hunt or fish because they have others who do this work for them?"

"Yes."

"We were also told that many whites do not make their own clothes."

"In the stone villages this is often the case, but people living outside them still make much of their own clothing."

A contemptuous snort reflected the Ute's opinion of the white way of life. "Your people sound very lazy to me."

"Pampered is more like it."

Two Owls scrutinized Nate's profile. "If life in the stone villages is so easy, why did you travel to the mountains to live?"

"I was tricked."

"How?"

"An uncle claimed he would give me a great treasure if I came, so I did. As it turned out, he did not own the kind of treasure I thought he did."

"You came for money?"

"Yes."

"I know about the money whites recieve for the beaver pelts they collect. Why are your people so interested in having something you cannot eat and cannot wear? What purpose does your money serve?"

"Whites like to own money for the same reasons Indians like to own horses. The more they have, the richer they are."

"But horses have a purpose. They can be ridden or used to haul belongings or eaten when game is scarce. What can you do with money?"

"Buy clothes and food and land."

"Ah. You use money to trade for things you want, much like we trade one thing for another, such as horses for a woman."

"Yes."

"Why not trade directly? Why use money at all?"

The persistent questions began to annoy Nate. He wanted to keep his mind on the task at hand, not be distracted by idle chatter about the white man's economic system. "Because money is easier to carry in a pocket than a horse," he replied.

Two Owls chuckled. "I think I understand now, but your ways still seem strange to me."

Nate made no sign, hoping the Ute would do the same. No such luck.

"Will you go back to the stone villages to live one day?"

"Not if I can help it. I like the mountains."

"What does your guardian spirit want you to do?"

"My what?"

"Your guardian spirit. You must have gone on a vision quest and talked to the spirit being who watches over you."

"I have no idea what you are talking about."

"Guardian spirits teach us proper prayers and songs to use when addressing the spirit world. They also reveal which objects are most sacred to us and will protect us from harm. Every Ute has a guardian spirit. If your people do not, it would explain a lot of things."

Nate recalled a passage from the Bible he'd read in Sunday School when a boy. Although he couldn't quote it, he remembered the general thrust. "Now I know what you mean. My people have another word for them. They call such things guardian"—he began in sign and finished in English—"angels."

"Angels?" Two Owls said awkwardly, rolling the word on his tongue.

Nate was going to repeat the word when a harsh screech of rage arose up ahead.

Chapter Ten

Two Owls reined his stallion to the left and
motioned while barking a few words in the Ute
tongue.

Turning the mare, Nate hurried into the trees,
leading the other horses into concealment. No sooner
did the last of the pack animals reach cover than
several figures appeared to the west, running along
the bank. Nate was stunned to see Thaddeus Baxter
out in front, pursued by two speedy Blackfeet. The
Ohioan was trying to escape!

Baxter raced awkwardly, his bound arms throwing
off his stride, but he maintained surprising speed
nonetheless. He glanced anxiously over his shoulder
again and again, desperation on his face.

For their part, the Blackfeet bounded like fleet
deer. One held a war club, another a bow. They were
confident of overtaking their quarry and did not
exert themselves to their utmost.

Nate wanted to shout, to let Baxter know he was
there, but such a move would have been foolish. The

other Blackfeet were sure to appear any second.

The Ohioan didn't get very far, 50 feet at most. He was looking back one more time when his left foot snagged in a clump of weeds and down he went, pitching onto his face and upper chest. Before he could do more than rise to his knees the Blackfeet were there, each grabbing an arm and brutally yanking him erect.

Damn the bastards all to hell! Nate thought, raising the Hawken, ready to fire if they acted as if they were going to kill Baxter. Hang the consequences! He couldn't just sit there and let the man be slain.

But the warriors only wheeled and half-pulled, half-dragged the feebly struggling trapper off.

How had Baxter managed to break away from them? Nate wondered. He watched until the trio was lost to view and glanced at the Ute. "That was close."

"We will let them get a ways ahead and follow their tracks."

"I am not much of a tracker."

Two Owls grinned. "I am one of the best in my village. We will not lose them."

Nate studied the warrior for a moment. "Will you help me save my friends?" he asked.

"I came back mainly to kill Blackfeet."

"Will you help me?" Nate repeated, puzzled as to why the Ute avoided the question.

"I will do what I can," Two Owls signed enigmatically.

They fell silent and stayed hidden for ten minutes, then moved out and trailed the war party. Nate noticed a somber, thoughtful expression on the Indian, but didn't pry. He was glad for the chance to think and plan. His best bet for freeing his friends would be late at night, when most or all of the Blackfeet should be asleep. But if they made forts every night, how could he get his friends out undetected? The problem seemed unsolvable.

For over an hour the tracks led west along the stream. Two Owls raised his right hand and halted when they reached a spot where the stream narrowed and the bank was low. He leaned over the side of his mount and scanned the soft earth intently, then straightened and pointed at the opposite side. "They have crossed here."

"Lead on," Nate said.

Due north was the new direction, over a series of hills and around the base of a snow-capped peak. The sun rose ever higher and the shadows in the narrow gorges and valleys lengthened.

Nate expected the band to stop now and then to rest, but the Blackfeet kept pushing on. Why were they in such a hurry? Simply to get home? Or did they have a rendezvous with another band planned? If the latter, his problems were compounded. Fourteen Blackfeet were more than enough. Any more and a rescue became virtually impossible.

The afternoon waxed and waned and the sun dipped toward the western horizon.

"They will halt soon to make camp for the night," Two Owls said.

"I hope so."

"Once they do, we must find a suitable spot to make our camp, somewhere we can safely build a fire."

"No fire."

"If we pick carefully they will never spot it."

"No fire. I have plenty of bear meat. We do not need to cook food."

Two Owls frowned and seemed about to argue the point. Instead he faced forward and made no comment.

Only half the sun was visible when the Blackfeet

finally halted for the night. They encamped in a ravine between two mountains where they were sheltered from the elements and secure from searching eyes.

Nate would never have known they were there if not for the Ute. The two of them were following the trail and were within a quarter of a mile of the ravine when Two Owls looked up to survey the countryside and spotted a pair of Blackfeet emerging from the erosion-caused defile; he halted and gestured for Nate to do the same.

With bows in hand, apparently going to hunt meat for their supper, the two Blackfeet headed westward into dense woodland.

Two Owls moved to the left and went four hundred yards, stopping in the shelter of a barren hillock. "This is as good a spot as any to stay tonight."

"Are we safe here?"

"As safe as anywhere else."

"I mean are we too close to the Blackfeet?"

"No. They will not stray far from their camp. We should build a fort or lean-to of our own to shield us from the wind. We are at a much higher elevation than we were this morning and the temperature can drop drastically by morning," Two Owls disclosed. "We would be better off with a fire."

"No fire."

"You are a stubborn man, Grizzly Killer."

Nate set about feeding the horses. There was no water nearby, but they had slaked their thirst at the stream earlier when they were crossing and that drink would have to tide them over until the morning. He hobbled them and removed the packs, took out a handful of dried meat, then stepped over to where the Ute sat at the base of a cottonwood tree. "Would you like some bear meat?"

"Yes."

Sharing the handful equally, Nate sat down and sighed. He chewed on a strip and contemplated his predicament.

"Do you know how you will save your friends yet?"

"No. Maybe you can help me with an idea. Tell me what the Blackfeet do between evening and dawn."

"That is easy. They make their forts first. Then some go after food using only bows or lances. Fusees are never fired in enemy territory for obvious reasons, except in an emergency. The game is cleaned and cooked, and after eating they sit around talking or singing until late."

"In this case they post guards all night to watch the prisoners?"

"Of course. They probably take turns."

"At what point during the night would most of them undoubtedly be asleep?"

"Shortly before dawn everyone except the guards will be sound asleep. Do you think you will make your try then?"

"Seems to be the best time," Nate said. "But I need a distraction to draw their attention and keep them busy."

"May I make a suggestion?"

"By all means."

"Fire."

"Set the forts on fire?"

"Unless you would prefer to set the entire forest on fire."

"I have already considered torching the forts and I think it would be too dangerous. My friends could be slain before I get to them."

"They will definitely be slain if you do not do something, and this is the best idea."

Nate mentally debated the merits of the scheme in depth. He couldn't ask for a better distraction. If the Blackfeet constructed three forts each night, he'd only have to set the two not containing his friends ablaze. The cries of the warriors inside would draw the guards from the third fort, and in the confusion of the flames and the smoke he might be able to get Shakespeare and Baxter out. "I think it is the best idea."

"I thought you would."

"What will you be doing while I am crawling up to the forts to set them on fire?"

The Ute laughed. "Why must you do everything the hard way?"

"I do not understand."

"If you try crawling right up to the forts and starting the fires there, the guards are bound to hear you. Why not light two torches and carry them behind you until you are close enough to set the forts on fire? The guards will not have time to react and the forts will swiftly be engulfed in flames. You can be in and out before the Blackfeet dogs have time to piss themselves."

Another excellent suggestion. Nate signed as much.

"My people have had many years of experience battling the Blackfeet. We have learned a few tricks in that time."

"The Utes are known far and wide as powerful fighters," Nate truthfully noted. "I am surprised the Blackfeet travel such a great distance to raid your villages."

"That is why they come."

"Again I do not understand."

Leaning against the trunk, Two Owls explained patiently. "The greater the enemy, the greater the glory. Why count coup on dogs when you can count them on panthers?"

"You are telling me the Blackfeet like to raid the Utes because they know your people are tough in warfare?"

"Yes. I do not know how it is with you whites, but Indians measure the might of a tribe by the might of its enemies. Do you ever hear of the Blackfeet raiding the Otos or the Iowas?''

"No," Nate admitted.

Two Owls grunted. "Because the Blackfeet would not soil their hands fighting such pathetic adversaries. The Otos, Iowas, and others are weak, and the Blackfeet will not stoop to granting such weaklings the distinction of being their enemies."

Nate was astonished by the information. No one had ever told him about this aspect of Indian affairs. "You almost sound like you admire the Blackfeet. I thought you hated them."

"I hate them, but I am wise enough to admire their fighting skill."

"Do all tribes share this philosophy?"

"Some. Not all. Only the best."

The man's proud boasting almost made Nate chuckle, but he wisely refrained. They ate for a while. Two Owls requested more meat, which Nate gladly provided. Twilight descended.

"One last time I will urge you to agree to a fire," the Ute said.

A nip already was in the air. Nate gazed at the snow crowning the mountains and felt a slight chill. Even with blankets, by morning they would be extremely uncomfortable. He glanced at the slope of the hillock, calculating. "I doubt the Blackfeet would see our smoke."

"They will not," Two Owls said, sitting forward, sensing victory. "I will build a lean-to and we will place the fire inside. Most of the smoke will be dispersed before it rises as high as the trees."

Nate had used the same trick once himself, against the Utes. He reluctantly nodded. "All right. Build your fire."

With enthusiastic alacrity Two Owls set up a sizeable lean-to and got a small fire going under-

neath, in the center. When satisfied with his handi-
work he sat back and rubbed his hands together over
the flickering flames. "I am glad you finally agreed.
I was afraid we would come to blows."

"Why?"

Two Owls looked at him. "If you had said no I was
going to build a fire anyway."

Nate couldn't help but laugh. He liked the man,
despite his arrogance.

"Will you try to rescue your friends tonight?"

"Since you know the ways of the Blackfeet better
than I do, what would you recommend?"

"I would wait until tomorrow night. The farther
they travel, the less of a chance they will be expecting
pursuit. You will take them completely by surprise."

"Do you think we could lose their trail tomorrow?"

"No. I can track a snake over solid rock. And there
is no bad weather to worry about."

"How do you know?"

Two Owls made a sweeping motion toward the
nearest peaks. "I have lived here all my life. I can
determine the weather we will have by the taste of
the air."

Lord, what a braggart! Nate nodded as if he
believed the statement, and stared at the forest.
Having another day worked out well, gave him time
to steel his nerves for the attempt. He felt confident
the Blackfeet would not harm his friends until then.
By the day after tomorrow the three of them would
be en route to his cabin. The beaver would have to
wait until another time. Next year, maybe.

"Grizzly Killer?"

"Yes?"

"How many coups have you counted?"

Nate cocked his head. Why ask such a personal
question? Then he recollected that warriors from
many tribes boasted of their exploits after the fact;

indeed, they were expected to relate the details to the entire tribe at special ceremonies. How many *had* he killed? He honestly couldn't recall. "I have lost count," he replied.

Two Owls was dumbfounded for a moment. He recovered his composure and leaned forward. "How can a man forget how many enemies he has killed?"

"My people do not keep track of such things."

"You do not count coup?"

"No."

Two Owls clucked and shook his head. "Truly you whites are a strange race. There must be a purpose for your existence, but I cannot imagine what it is. You do not seem to know anything about the right way to live. When I tell my people all I have learned, they will think I exaggerated."

"You?" Nate responded, and hid his broad grin by feeding a branch to the flames.

Chapter Eleven

The next day began with a flurry of activity.

A strong hand shaking Nate's right shoulder awoke him before the sun appeared on the eastern horizon. Stars still dominated the heavens. Blinking in momentary confusion, he looked up at Two Owls, then sat and rubbed his eyes. A nip in the air made him shiver. "What is it?"

"What do you think? We must be ready to leave by sunrise."

"But this early?"

"Would you rather they started without us?"

Nate recalled the frantic search of the day before and shook his head. "I will be ready quickly." He threw off his blanket, noticed the fire had dwindled to smoldering embers, and stretched. His first priority was relieving his bladder; then he attended to loading the packs on the horses and preparing the mare for travel. Checking all his guns came next. The Ute made no effort to help and Nate wasn't about to ask. A rosy glow painted the sky in the east by the time he finished.

"No wonder the Blackfeet got a head start on you yesterday," Two Owls joked. "You take half a day just getting ready to leave."

Grinning more out of courtesy than any keen appreciation of the Ute's sense of humor, Nate went to the fire and stomped it out. He climbed on the mare and signed, "After you."

Two Owls rode slowly around the hillock until he had a clear view of the ravine. He held up his hand and halted.

Pushing against the stirrups so he could stand in the saddle, Nate was able to see the country beyond. He involuntarily stiffened at the sight of Shakespeare and Baxter being pushed and prodded northward. Both men were ringed by Blackfeet; apparently the band had no intention of letting a repeat of yesterday's escape attempt occur. At their head walked White Bear.

Not until the war party disappeared in the distance did Two Owls goad his stallion forward.

Nate arched his spine to alleviate stiffness in his lower back, and resigned himself to another day of tedious tracking. His inner thighs ached from all the riding he'd done, which gave him a little added incentive to free his friends. In his mind's eye he reviewed his plans for the rescue, going over it again and again, plotting for contingencies.

By mid-morning the temperature had climbed into the sixties. By noon the sun shone down mercilessly on the two of them and their animals and the air hung like a sweltering, heavy robe over the landscape.

Nate wiped perspiration from his brow with the sleeve of his buckskins and longed for a drink. He hadn't realized it could get so hot at the higher elevations. They were skirting a mountain on their right. Overhead an eagle soared. He wished he had the bird's vantage point so he could scan the horizon for water.

Not much later they came to a small lake. Two Owls stopped and studied the shore, then rode boldly to the edge of the bank and slid off his horse.

Uncertain whether they should expose themselves so brazenly, Nate reluctantly rode to the lake and dismounted. His eyes roved over the shore on each side and saw no evidence of the band.

The Ute noticed and chuckled. "We are safe, Grizzly Killer. The Blackfeet passed this way much earlier."

"What if they're resting on the north shore? They could see us."

Two Owls nodded at the ground. "They rested here for a while, then hurried on. Remember, they want ot reach their village as quickly as they can so they can show off their prisoners. Their people will celebrate the capture of your friends for days."

"Not if I can help it." Nate let the mare drink and knelt to splash some refreshing moisture on his face. When she finished he dropped prone and greedily gulped until he couldn't take another drop. As he straightened he saw the warrior regarding him critically.

"You should not drink so much at one time. When going long periods without water it is better to drink in moderation when the opportunity arises."

"You concentrate on the Blackfeet and I will take care of my drinking."

"As you wish. But do not bother to complain if your stomach aches shortly."

"My stomach is fine," Nate declared testily.

A half hour later his stomach disagreed. They had ridden two miles from the lake when he felt an acute spasm and almost doubled over. Thankfully the Ute was in front and couldn't see his discomfort. The pain mystified him. He'd drunk equally as much on other occasions, so why should he have trouble now?

Before them lay a verdant meadow. A buck stood to the northwest, chewing contentedly, undisturbed by their presence. From a cluster of boulders to the east several groundhogs stood erect and studied them before one of the creatures uttered a shrill cry and they all darted into their burrows.

Nate gritted his teeth and patiently weathered his bellyache. The spasms grew progressively worse for 15 minutes, then abruptly abated. He mentally vowed never to drink so much again. Ever.

The terrain consisted of rolling hills sandwiched between regal mountains. In the distance to the north reared a bald peak that strongly resembled a human skull in its general outline. They made directly toward it, and the closer they came the more realistic the imaginary skull appeared.

"That is Dead Man's Mountain," Two Owls revealed, indicating the peak with a jerk of his thumb. "My people consider it to be bad medicine."

"Why?"

"Once three Utes went up the mountain to catch eagles and pluck their feathers. Two of the men were never seen again. The third stumbled into our village, said, 'The big hairy thing,' and died."

"The big hairy thing?"

Two Owls nodded, twisting so his gestures could be seen better. "That is what he told the man who caught him as he fell to the ground."

"What was he referring to?"

"We have no idea."

"A grizzly maybe?"

"If a grizzly had attacked him, he would have said so."

"Were there claw marks on him?" Nate asked.

"None. No marks at all. Our medicine man

believed he saw something that frightened him so badly it scared him to death."

Nate chuckled. "And you believe this story?"

"Yes. It happened in my great-grandfather's time and he saw the man who died. When I was a child he told the tale to me and swore it was true."

Lifting his right hand over his eyes to shield them away from the sunlight, Nate scrutinized the mountain. "There must be a logical explanation," he commented after a minute.

Two Owls slowed so he could ride even with the youth. "Why?"

"Because there are logical explanations for everything."

"Do all whites believe this?"

"Most do, yes."

"Then most whites are fools. There are matters men will never understand. The ways of spirit beings, for instance, are beyond our power to comprehend."

"Are these the same guardian spirits you were talking about before?"

"Those and many others," Two Owls said, and motioned at the atmosphere. "The spirit beings who live all around us. Surely you have talked to one?"

"Not recently."

"Go on a vision quest sometime. You will see what I mean."

"One day," Nate signed noncommittally, inwardly laughing at the notion of communicating with unseen spirits.

"Have you ever seen a lake monster?" the Ute unexpectedly inquired.

"There are no such things."

Two Owls adopted an exasperated expression. "There are men in my tribe who have seen them, so do not sit there and tell me such creatures do not exist."

"Can you blame me for being skeptical? I would have to see one myself before I could believe such an outrageous yarn."

"Go to Bear Lake. A monster lives in the water and is seen often."

"I have been there. The last rendezvous was held on the south shore, and not one person reported seeing any monster," Nate signed with all the patience he could muster.

"No wonder. There were too many people there and the monster stayed in hiding at the bottom of the lake."

"How convenient."

"If you do not believe me, ask the Shoshones."

Nate straightened and studied the warrior's features. Two Owls had no way of knowing he was married to a Shoshone so the remark had been made innocently. "Why them?"

"They live in the vicinity of Bear Lake and they know all about the monster. A woman we captured told us all about it. The beast is like a great serpent but has short legs and sometimes crawls out onto the land. She also told us the monster sprays water out of its mouth."

"Was she suffering from a blow on the head at the time?"

Hissing in anger, Two Owls rode several yards in front of the mare.

Nate grinned and shook his head in amazement. How could any sane person believe such nonsense. When he returned to his cabin he would ask Winona about the so-called monster, and he felt certain she would laugh and agree with him that the woman had concocted the entire story. Lake monster indeed!

They continued tracking the Blackfeet in strained silence. Two Owls did not ask another question the remainder of the day. Only when the sun completed its transit of the sky and evening was almost upon them did he deign to look at Nate.

"We should make camp soon."

"Pick a spot. I trust your judgment," Nate responded, and realized he'd made a mistake when the Ute's lips compressed.

They had been rising steadily for the better part of an hour, and above them loomed a ragged ridge. Two Owls rode to just below it and slid from his horse. He stepped higher and peered at whatever lay above, then motioned for Nate to join him.

Gripping the Hawken in his left hand, Nate moved next to the warrior and gazed out over a plateau stretching for three or four miles. In the foreground was a level, grassy field covering 20 to 30 acres. Across the field lay a pond, then dense forest. And erecting their forts on the north side of the pond were the Blackfeet.

"They have selected their campsite wisely," Two Owls noted. "To get close enough to hurl your torches will require great stealth."

Nate said nothing. He'd already perceived as much and was plotting his approach.

"I could do it for you."

Surprised, Nate turned. "The job is mine. They are my friends."

"True, but I can move quieter than any white ever born. My chances of success are better than yours."

"Thank you, but no. I will do the task myself."

"As you wish."

They walked to their horses and led them lower into a stand of pine trees.

"Tonight we will not use a fire," Two Owls stated.

Nodding absently, Nate started to remove a pack from his pack horse.

"What are you doing?" Two Owls asked.

"Unloading the . . ." Nate lowered his arms as

comprehension dawned. They might need to make a swift escape, in which case there wouldn't be time to strap all the packs on the animals. Although the horses were tired and deserved their rest, he had to leave them fully burdened until the rescue of his friends was achieved. He tightened the pack and reclined against a nearby tree.

Two Owls strolled over. "You should use what light is left to spy on the Blackfeet and plan your strategy."

"I will soon. Thanks."

The Ute squatted and scratched his chest. "Do you have a wife, Grizzly Killer?"

"Yes," Nate replied, wondering why the warrior asked such a question.

"Do you have children?"

"Not yet."

"Have as many as you can. Children are the sweetest blessings of the Great Mystery."

"I had no idea the Utes were such devoted parents," Nate signed. The Ute glowered and began to rise, so he quickly added, "I was complimenting your people, not insulting them."

Two Owls eased down again. "Children are the legacy we leave for future generations. They are more precious than the finest hides." He paused. "I was told once that whites hit their children to punish them. Is this true?"

Nate thought of the beatings his own father had administered when he was younger. "Yes."

Revulsion rippled over the Ute's countenance. "How disgusting. We never hit our children. There are better methods to use when instructing them in proper behavior. When you hit a child, you hurt the child's soul."

"I will try to remember that when I have my own children."

"Since you do not pray to your guardian spirit, how do you contact the spirit world?"

What was all this leading up to? Nate wondered. He signed, "Whites usually pray directly to the Great Mystery."

"Then I will do the same for you."

"I do not understand."

"Even though you are a white, I like you, Grizzly Killer. If you are killed tonight, I will pray to the Great Mystery on your behalf and ask that the passage of your soul from this world to the next be swift and safe."

"Thank you," Nate signed, and meant it.

Chapter Twelve

Sleeping was impossible. Nate tried to get some rest, but couldn't. He lay on his back on a patch of soft grass and covered himself with a blanket, then spent about an hour tossing and turning and staring at the stars. Finally he gave the notion up as a lost cause, replaced the blanket in a pack, and sat down close to the Ute, who still sat under the tree. Without a fire they could barely see one another, so he had to pay particular attention when the warrior used sign language.

"Are you ready?"

"Yes. I want to get it over with."

"Be patient. Do not try to rush or you will be killed. As much as I despise the Blackfeet, I must admit they are excellent fighters."

"I plan to sneak past them into the woods north of the pond, make a small fire where it cannot be seen, and light two torches. Then I will set the forts ablaze. The rest will be in the Great Mystery's hands."

Two Owls grunted. "Your plan is a good one. I will

take cover in the field of grass and kill any Blackfeet who try to stop you."

"Just be certain you do not shoot my friends or me by mistake."

The Ute grinned. "When I shoot someone, Grizzly Killer, it is never by mistake."

They engaged in small talk to pass the time. Nate was surprised to learn the Utes had not always been noted for their warlike tendencies. Many years ago, before the coming of the Spaniards, the Utes lived in small family groups. They spent most of their time in the high mountain valleys seeking fish, berries, and game. When the weather turned cold they would follow the buffalo and antelope to the south and stay there until spring.

But the advent of the Spanish changed Ute life forever. The simple hunters and seed gatherers obtained horses and became expert horsemen. The family groups banded together and began conducting raids on Spanish settlements and other tribes. In short order the Utes were expert marauders, ranging far and wide to count coup, steal more horses, and plunder at will.

Soon the Utes were in contention with other powerful tribes: the Cheyenne, Arapaho, Comanche, and Kiowa. They held their own against all of them. Only one other tribe successfully conducted raids into Ute territory on a regular basis. The Blackfeet.

Nate found it hard to conceive of the Utes as seed gatherers and peaceful hunters, and he marveled at the fact that possession of horses should make such a big difference in their lives. Granted, horses gave the tribes greater mobility than ever before and enabled those who possessed mounts to have an unfair advantage in battle, but he couldn't understand the drastic change.

Two Owls plied Nate with questions about life in

the white man's world. How many whites were there? How many stone villages? How many horses did the Great Chief of all the whites own? How many coups had the Great Chief counted?

Nate answered honestly, and was annoyed when many of his answers were greeted with smiles. The Utes found it incredible that there were ten million people in the United States, and that in one village alone, New York City, there were over 125,000. He found it humorous Nate didn't know the number of horses owned by the President. And he laughed at learning the Great Chief did not count coup after the Indian fashion.

Midnight came and went. The night grew progressively cooler. Wolves howled and panthers screamed. A strong breeze from the northwest rattled the trees.

Despite the late hour, Nate felt no fatigue. Nervousness assailed him, and he had to force his arms and legs to stay still. He glanced time and again at the sky, especially the eastern horizon, gauging the passage of the stars, and tried not to dwell on the job he must do.

They had settled into a mutually reflective silence for a long while when Two Owls gazed overhead, cleared his throat, and signed, "It is time."

Nate stood and hefted the Hawken. "Then I will be on my way."

"Do you have what is necessary to start the fire?"

"In my pouch," Nate assured him, and looked into the warrior's eyes. "Be careful."

"You too."

They climbed to the summit of the plateau and headed due north, moving quietly through the tall grass. Once a large animal, possibly a deer, snorted and ran off. They crouched and waited a suitable interval before resuming their approach, reaching the south shore of the pond safely.

Nate knelt and parted the grass to stare across the oval body of water. He estimated it to be 60 feet in diameter. The three forts were easy to distinguish due to their unnatural conical shape. Not a glimmer of light showed inside any of them. He glanced at the Ute, gave a wave, and bore to the right, swinging wide around the pond until he attained the sanctuary of the woods.

In order to avoid being heard or seen, Nate traveled a good 30 yards before he stumbled on a narrow gully that would suit his purposes ideally. He gathered limbs from under several trees, piled them at the bottom of the gully, and opened his pouch to remove his flint and steel. Next he broke a few twigs into small pieces to use as kindling and added three pinches of coarse black powder from his powder horn to serve as tinder.

On only the fifth strike to the flint on the steel did the sparks ignite the powder, which flashed and sparked and in turn ignited the kindling. A few strategically placed puffs and the kindling caught, the flames growing rapidly, and soon the limbs were burning and crackling.

Now Nate had to hurry. He scoured his immediate vicinity for a pair of suitable makeshift torches, and found two stout broken pine limbs that would suffice. Cradling the rifle under his left arm, he used his butcher knife to strip off the shoots and seized each limb by its thin end. Rising, he held the thick ends in the flames until both caught.

Clambering from the gully with two makeshift torches in his hands proved difficult, but he managed. Bending at the waist, he ran sideways while keeping the torches low to the ground. When he had gone two thirds of the way to the pond he turned with his back to the south and moved backwards, his body hopefully screening the torches from

enemy eyes. Not that he expected many of the
Blackfeet to be awake. Perhaps those guarding his
friends were, but the rest should be sound asleep.

He tripped and corrected his balance in the nick
of time. One of the limbs sputtered as if on the verge
of going out. With bated breath he waited until the
flames burned brightly, then hastened onward, his
head twisted so he could see any obstacles.

The forts had been erected in a row, from west to
east, spaced ten feet apart. As before, the Blackfeet
had placed Shakespeare and Baxter in the middle
structure. Earlier, Nate had watched as his friends
were shoved inside and followed by a pair of
Blackfeet.

Please let there be only two in the fort still! he
prayed as he drew within 20 feet of the inky shapes
and paused to gird himself. He must not slow down
for even a second once he burst from cover. To stand
still would be to die.

So far no sound at all issued from the forts.

Nate clamped his arm down harder on the
Hawken, gripped the limbs more securely, whirled,
and charged, his moccasins smacking on the pine
needles and soft earth underfoot. Go! he goaded
himself. Go! Go!

He sped from the forest and reached the wester-
most fort. Instantly he propped the torch against it,
letting the flames lick at the poles, and dashed to the
fort to the east, repeating the procedure. He stood
back to watch the structure catch, then ran around
to the front, gripping the rifle in both hands.

Not a sound issued from the structures. All the
Blackfeet were evidently still slumbering.

Nate ran to the middle fort and stood to the right
of the doorway, waiting. His body tingled in expecta-
tion. Soon. They had to notice the flames soon.

They did. Loud screeches arose in the west fort,

followed moments later by shouts in the east one. A warrior in the middle fort shouted something in the Blackfeet language.

Bracing his legs, Nate gripped the Hawken by the barrel and focused on the waist-high doorway. What's taking them so long? he wondered in amazement. They should be bolting out of there like frightened rabbits. He detected motion out of the corner of his eye and looked up.

A Blackfoot was emerging from the west fort, a war club clutched in his right hand. He glanced around, spied the youth, and vented a war whoop as he sprang erect. No sooner did he stand, however, than an arrow flashed out of the night and thudded into his chest, the impact spinning him to the left. He blinked, stared mutely at the feathers jutting from his body, and pitched over.

Distracted by the man's death, Nate didn't realize someone was scrambling from the fort at his very feet until he heard a feral hiss and glanced down in consternation to see a burly Blackfoot about to bury a tomahawk in his legs. He threw himself backward, barely evading the blow, then swung the heavy Hawken like a club and clipped the Indian on the jaw.

The Blackfoot sagged, still conscious but dazed. Nate kicked him, delivering the tip of his right moccasin to the point of the warrior's chin. Teeth crunched and the Blackfoot collapsed. Bending forward, Nate grabbed the man by the shoulders and heaved, pulling the warrior all the way out.

More and more yells of alarm were voiced as the rest of the war party awakened. A second Blackfoot exited the fort to the west, and promptly received a shaft in his jugular for the effort.

From Nate's rear arose a ghastly shriek, and he twisted to observe yet another warrior who had just stepped outside and been greeted by the lethal flight of an arrow into his left eye. The Blackfoot grabbed at the shaft, sagged against the poles, and toppled over.

Grayish-white smoke billowed upward from the pair of burning forts. Already poles were ablaze.

Another warrior started to crawl from the middle fort.

Nate looked down, intending to club this one as he had the other, saving his balls for when they would really be needed. He found himself staring down the barrel of a fusee angled awkwardly in the direction of his head, and his immediate reaction was to jerk to the right, diving for the ground.

The fusee went off, booming like a cannon, narrowly missing him. Fusees were trade guns distributed by the Hudson's Bay Company and others, inferior smooth-bored flintlocks that were no match for the rifled arms of the trappers at long range but were decidedly deadly close up.

Nate returned the favor the moment his shoulder struck the earth, leveling the Hawken at the warrior's enraged face and sending a ball boring into the man's brain. He pushed to his feet and quickly dragged the Indian aside, then dropped to one knee and peered into the gloomy interior. "Shakespeare?"

"We're here, son. Hurry. Our arms and legs are tied."

Hastening inside, Nate dimly perceived the prone forms of his friends. He drew his butcher knife and set to work while listening to the bellows of the Blackfeet as they communicated back and forth. Had any more tried to escape the burning forts and been transfixed by arrows?

"Thank God you've come!" Baxter declared. "I'd about given us up for dead."

"Don't dawdle," Shakespeare advised. "I speak a little of the Blackfoot tongue. They're frantic because every warrior who has stepped outside has been killed, and they're getting set to pour out all at once before it's too late."

Nate appreciated the warning. Two Owls could not possibly cover both forts simultaneously and prevent all the Blackfeet from reaching cover. He sliced off the leather strips binding Shakespeare's wrists and ankles, then turned to Baxter.

"Please hurry," the Ohioan pleaded.

"Who is out there doing the killing?" Shakespeare asked, moving to the doorway. "Did you meet another trapper?"

"No. It's a friend of mine. A Ute."

"A Ute!" Baxter exclaimed. "They're as bad as the Blackfeet."

"I'll be damned," Shakespeare said, and chuckled.

Baxter went on in a rush. "Where did you meet a Ute? How do we know he can be trusted? They're heathen like all the rest."

With a final slash of his knife Nate freed the Ohioan and slid the knife in its sheath. He ignored the questions and moved to the doorway. "This is no time for talking. Stay close to me and we'll get out of this alive." He gave each of them one of his flint-locks even though his rifle was unloaded.

"The Blackfeet are awful quiet all of a sudden," Shakespeare noted.

Nate realized the band had stopped shouting. They must be about to make their bid, he deduced, and gambled on beating them to the high grass. "Follow me!" he cried, and darted through the doorway. He angled to the right, planning to skirt the pond and plunge into the field. He had to go past the west fort to do so, which was now fully ablaze on the side nearest the forest. As he came abreast of the doorway he glanced down.

Suddenly Blackfeet poured from the fort, four all

told, one after the other in a mad scramble to flee the flames. The first one saw Nate, voiced a fierce roar, and lunged.

The warrior's fingers just touched Nate's right leg as he went by and spurred him to go faster. Nate cast a hasty glance over his shoulder and saw Baxter fire at close range into the warrior's head. Then all three of them were past the forts and racing for their lives.

More Blackfeet emerged from the east fort. One of them was hit squarely in the neck by an arrow, but the rest were on their feet in a heartbeat and gave chase, uttering savage whoops.

Where was Two Owls? Nate wondered, his legs pumping. Only ten feet separated him from the tall grass, ten feet to possible safety, when a Blackfoot arrow struck him.

Chapter Thirteen

The shaft caught Nate in the back, in the right side just below the ribs, lancing his body with sheer torment and causing him to stumble and almost fall. If Shakespeare and Baxter hadn't paused to assist him, he would have gone down and been at the mercy of the Blackfeet. But sturdy hands seized him by the upper arms and propelled him the remaining distance to the field.

Shock made Nate dizzy and he nearly dropped his rifle. Only vaguely was he conscious of doing his best to keep up, running mechanically, struggling to recover his composure. If he didn't, he'd die. Think! Use your brain and think!

"Keep going, son," Shakespeare said.

"We won't let go of you," Baxter added.

But Nate knew they must. The Blackfeet would overtake them easily otherwise. He lowered his right hand and felt the bloody stone tip of the arrow protruding two or three inches from his flesh. Had it punctured a vital organ? He couldn't tell, and he couldn't stop to examine the wound until the three of them eluded the Blackfeet.

"They're gaining," Baxter said.

Clarity abruptly returned. Nate was conscious of his driving legs and his thudding heart. He suppressed the pain and declared, "Let go."

"Not yet," the mountain man replied.

"Let go of me," Nate insisted. "I can manage. I'm only slowing you down."

"No," Shakespeare said.

"Are you sure?" Baxter asked.

"Let go," Nate reiterated, and twisted to wrench himself from their grasp. His brashness threw all three of them off stride, but they stayed erect and sprinted on into the night in a weaving pattern. Gritting his teeth, he looked back once more and spotted the warriors fanning out, the nearest 20 feet away.

"Which way?" Baxter asked.

"South," Nate answered in a raspy tone. "Our horses are below the rim."

For another minute the marathon of death continued. Nate fell a few feet behind his companions. His buckskin shirt became drenched with his blood, and the rubbing motion of the shaft inside his body produced intense nausea. It felt as if someone had their finger inside of him, poking around carelessly, and he wanted so badly to scream in anguish. But he couldn't. Not now. He must be strong. He must have the stamina of a bull or be slaughtered like a cow.

"They're still gaining," Baxter said anxiously.

Again Nate glanced at their pursuers and made an impulsive decision. Perhaps they would have a better chance if they didn't stay together. If each one of them only had two or three Blackfeet after them, the odds were better they would escape. In his agony the idea seemed logical and he told the others, "Split up!"

"No!" Shakespeare responded.

But Nate had already slanted to the right, his right hand grasping the arrow to hold it steady, the grass swishing as the blades parted before him. His right side hurt terribly and grew worse the farther he fled. In his excruciating torment he lost all sense of direction, all sense of the distance he traveled. He simply ran and weaved, ran and weaved, and when he finally drew up short it was to gape in astonishment at a wall of trees blocking his path.

The forest?

It couldn't be the forest! He should be at the southern rim with the horses waiting below. Unless —and the insight chilled his soul—unless he had gone the wrong way.

He looked to the east and, sure enough, there were the blazing forts. He was 40 yards from them, confounded by his own stupidity. Turning, grimacing as he did, he spied a bounding figure 30 feet off.

A Blackfoot!

In a panic he spun and dashed among the trees, afraid of crashing into a trunk and aggravating his wound. He ran until his breath came in ragged gasps and the pain in his side had spread to his chest and abdomen. He ran until he could run no more, and then he collapsed onto his knees and doubled over, biting his lips to suppress a groan.

Lord, he hurt!

Nate tried to quiet his breathing and listened, hearing nothing to indicate the Blackfeet were still after him. Sweat caked his skin from head to toe. Even his hair was soaked. He gingerly felt the arrow, and pushed a finger through the tear in his buckskin shirt to gingerly touch the surprisingly neat edge of the hole. To his immense relief the blood flow seemed to have ceased. Perhaps he wouldn't bleed to death after all.

He straightened with much difficulty and pondered his next move. First and foremost the arrow must come out. If he kept running with the shaft inside, the friction might tear open a crucial vein or rupture an untouched organ. But how could he remove it without assistance?

A means occurred to him, but he balked at attempting so grueling a task. Successive waves of agony convinced him to try, and he placed his Hawken at his side and reached his right arm behind his back. His fingers contacted the smooth feathers and he closed his hand around the thin shaft. Did he dare go through with it? Taking a deep breath, he steeled his sinews, then snapped his arm upward, trying to break the arrow.

Exquisite torture racked his entire being. His spine arched and he opened his mouth to scream, choking the cry in his throat, venting a gurgling whine. He thought for a moment he might pass out, but didn't. Don't give up! he chided himself. Try again.

Nate tightened his grip, tensed, fought off a brief attack of vertigo, and duplicated the snapping motion, putting all of his strength into the act. Through pounding waves of soul-wrenching misery he distinctly heard the crack, and his hand came around holding the broken section. He stared at the feathers, waiting for his head to clear, marveling that he had succeeded halfway. The worst was yet to come.

Tossing the piece to the ground, Nate clutched the front of the arrow just below the point with both hands and girded himself for the second phase. Please let me make it, he prayed. Slowly, so as not to tear his insides more than they already were, he pulled on the shaft, drawing it from the hole, the sickening sensation making him shudder violently. He had to pause and catch his breath, composing his nerves, then tried again. A revolting squishing noise accompanied the extraction, and it took all of his self-control to keep going. When at last the shaft came clear, he closed his eyes and doubled over.

Now what should he do? Think, Nate! Think. The wisest course seemed to be to head back to the rim and find his friends. They would treat the wound and bandage him. He was cetainly in no condition to take care of himself, and he didn't want to wander around in the forest with bloodthirsty Blackfeet hunting his scalp.

Nate waited for his strength to return, breathing shallowly, leery of passing out. He envisioned Winona's beautiful features, and recalled the gentle feel of her loving hands on his naked body. More than anything else in the world he wanted to see her again, to hold her in his arms and taste her lips on his own. Thinking about her soothed him, made him appreciate the fact he was still alive, still able to fight, to escape.

At length he roused from his reflection and shoved to his feet. His sides protested the movement, and he pressed his right elbow on the hole as he shuffled back toward the field. He must be careful. The Blackfeet were around somewhere.

Perhaps he should find a hiding place and stay there until daylight? The idea appealed to him, but his desire to rejoin Shakespeare and Baxter overrode his common sense.

Nate walked unsteadily toward the field. He could see the forts over a hundred yards away, burning so brightly they were undoubtedly visible for many miles. With them to orient him, he had no difficulty determining in which direction to travel. Unfortunately, his legs were endowed with a mind of their own. They longed to rest. For that matter, his entire body wanted to curl into a ball and not move for a year. Annoyed at his weakness, he branded his body a traitor and willed it to keep going.

He checked the wound as he walked. The exit hole exuded a trickle of blood but the entry hole wasn't bleeding at all. Perhaps he wouldn't need to cauterize.

Off in the distance a shot sounded.

Nate halted, listening for additional discharges. Had that been a rifle, a flintlock, or a fusee? He guessed it came from the end of the plateau. Maybe the Blackfeet were trying to take the horses! He hurried, or attempted to, but his body stubbornly refused to obey his mental commands. He mopped his brow with his left hand, and stopped in mid-stride when his negligence dawned.

He'd forgotten the Hawken!

Stunned by his stupidity, Nate turned and headed back. How could he forget the most essential piece of equipment a mountaineer owned? Sure, he was hurting, but pain was no excuse for being recklessly careless.

He came to the spot where he thought he'd extracted the arrow but saw no sign of the pieces or his rifle. Confused, he searched in an ever-widening circle. Every second of delay made him increasingly impatient.

After a minute Nate decided he was wrong, that he'd pulled out the arrow farther north, and trudged a dozen yards to search again. Still nothing. Exasperated, he went another dozen yards, and another, and each time he failed to locate the Hawken.

Fatigue and the stress to his system caused him to trip twice. He became intermittently dizzy, and worried he would pass out. His right foot bumped into a log. Sighing, he sat down and clutched his side.

Another shot cracked to the south.

Nate looked up. The damn Blackfeet must still be after his companions or Two Owls. He longed desperately to help them, and the motivation sufficed to bring him to his feet. To give up while breath remained was inconceivable. He'd continue on until he dropped from exhaustion.

Five minutes later he had yet to locate the rifle. His resolve evaporated like dew under the morning sun. Doubt plagued him. Doubt he could recover the Hawken. Doubt he would see Shakespeare again. Doubt he would ever again experience Winona's tender caress. His mental and emotional states fluctuated as rapidly as the breeze.

On the verge of collapsing, moving each foot with supreme effort, his eyes downcast, Nate was stepping over the rifle before he realized it was indeed there. Grinning, he grunted and bent down to reclaim his weapon. Vertigo assailed him and he sank to his knees.

A minute or so and he'd be fine. Just a minute. His chin sagged and he licked his exceptionally dry lips.

Somewhere nearby a twig snapped.

Nate's head snapped up and he froze, his ears straining to their limit, expecting to hear the muffled tread of moccasin-covered feet or a whispered phrase in the Blackfoot tongue. He shifted position quietly to grab the rifle. The gun was empty but he could still employ it as a club, and if Fate granted him the time he could reload.

A heavy silence hung over the forest.

Were there Blackfeet close at hand or were his frayed nerves playing a trick on him? Nate surveyed the woods and saw nothing to alarm him. He had begun to believe he was exaggerating the danger when the soft crunch of a footstep off to his left confirmed he wasn't alone.

Nate eased down on his left side, wincing at the discomfort, and glued his unblinking eyes on the forest. He instinctively knew it wasn't his friends come looking for him. The Blackfeet, true to their persistent natures, had not stopped searching for him.

Something moved, a shadow among shadows.

He perceived the outline of a man, an Indian, 15 yards off and heading cautiously northward. Whether the warrior carried a bow, lance, club, or fusee was irrelevant. In his state Nate was no match for an infant let alone a robust scalper of white men.

Nate scarcely breathed, watching the Blackfoot cross his line of vision and disappear in the trees. He halfheartedly wished he had not given his pistols to the others. Several times the warrior glanced in his direction but failed to spot him.

Full comprehension of his predicament hit him with the force of an avalanche. Although he'd always known in the back of his mind that he could die at any time, he was now closer to death than he'd ever been. If the wound didn't kill him, the Blackfeet would. The reality sank into the core of his being and chilled his blood.

Nate listened for the longest time, wanting to make certain the Indian had departed before trying to flee. To rise required a herculean exertion. He tottered, mulling whether to reload the rifle, and realized the chore would take more time than he could afford to spare. Using the Hawken as a crutch to prevent him from falling, he turned and hiked toward the field.

Luck might be on his side, he consoled himself. If most of the Blackfeet were off after Shakespeare and Baxter, and the one after him had missed him in the dark, he should be able to get to the horses without difficulty. All he had to do was stay on his feet.

Was that all?

He opened his mouth to laugh aloud, but checked himself in time. The indiscretion startled him. Was he so befuddled that he would betray his presence so foolishly?

Perspiration coated his brow as he channeled all of his concentration into reaching the field. Take it easy, he admonished himself. Take it one step at a time. That was all. One measly step. The field wasn't all that far. In minutes the single steps would add up to the distance he needed to cover. Just keep going no matter what the cost.

No matter what.

An eternity seemed to pass before all those steps ultimately did bring him to the edge of the forest, and he crouched behind a tree to catch his breath. To the east, 30 yards distant, burned the forts. Somehow, probably from sparks, the middle fort had been touched off and was burning furiously. Combined, the forts radiated light over the tall grass and into the adjacent forest.

Nate surmised he might see a few Blackfeet moving about, but there were none. His gaze raked the field repeatedly. Not so much as a single blade moved unnaturally. Even so, he hesitated, preferring to stay right where he was for the time being. He was temporarily safe. Why increase the odds of being spotted by leaving the sanctuary of the forest?

His fluttering eyelids answered the question. If he keeled over he would be at the mercy of the Blackfeet, other predators, and the weather. As long as he kept moving, he'd be all right. Which was easier said than accomplished.

Nate used tree limbs to pull himself up and stood stiffly, then hobbled into the grass that bordered the very edge of the trunks. Despite the anguish he stayed hunched over, ignoring the pain in his lower back. What was one more pain to a man trapped in a living nightmare, a hell worse than the Inferno?

His guardian angel must have been watching over him because he crossed the field without being attacked. The sight of the rim expanded his heart with joy and he walked the final five yards without the aid of the rifle. Soon he would be with his companions!

Nate stepped to the edge and halted, scanning the trees below, beaming in triumph that proved to be premature the very next instant when onrushing footsteps sounded to his rear and he twisted in horror to see a Blackfoot holding a war club aloft, a club that smashed into his right temple and sent him sailing from the plateau. The last coherent thought he had was inanely sublime; he hoped there were no Blackfeet in the hereafter.

Chapter Fourteen

Why did he feel as if he was in a boat being rocked violently by huge waves?

The sensation surprised him. He'd thought the afterlife would be different; at the very least it wouldn't be so dark. He couldn't see a blessed thing. Then he became aware of a hand on his left shoulder, shaking him rudely, and realized he wasn't dead after all but alive and simply had his eyes closed. Alive! The word echoed in his brain like the joyous peals of church bells.

The pain engulfed him a second later and brought him back to reality. Groaning, he opened his eyes, and he knew he might have been better off being dead because staring balefully down at him was a tall Blackfoot, the one who carried the Spanish sword, the warrior named White Bear.

Other Blackfeet materialized above and around him, most with malevolent expressions.

Nate didn't move or speak. Anything he did might provoke them. He scanned their painted faces and saw one of the warriors holding his rifle and wearing his bullet pouch and powder horn. If his hazy memory served, it was the same Blackfoot who had struck him with the war club.

White Bear growled a string of words in his language.

Still Nate stayed immobile.

Lashing out angrily, White Bear hit him across the face and barked more Blackfoot words.

The blow stung wickedly. Nate suppressed his rage and shook his head to signify he did not understand.

White Bear turned and addressed one of the warriors. They conversed for a bit, then White Bear looked at Nate and his hands signed a question: "Do you know sign language, white man?"

Nate hesitated. Should he admit his knowledge of not? A second slap prompted him to reveal he could use sign, if only to buy time, to delay his eventual torture. "Yes, White Bear."

Astonishment lined the Blackfoot's visage. "How do you know my name?"

Instead of telling the truth, Nate responded, "Every trapper has heard of the mighty Blackfoot warrior who wears a sword."

The false claim sparked a brief debate among the Blackfeet until White Bear silenced them with a wave of his arm.

"How are you known?"

"I am Grizzly Killer."

Several of the warriors laughed.

"How did one so young earn such a name?" White Bear asked, smirking.

"By killing grizzlies."

More mirth greeted the assertion.

White Bear did not appreciate the humor. "Where are your friends?" he demanded gruffly.

"I do not know," Nate replied, elated to learn the

frontiersman, the Ohioan, and the Ute were safe.

"Lie to me and I will cut out your tongue," White Bear vowed.

"I have no idea," Nate insisted, refusing to be cowed. "We were separated last night during the fight."

"The fight was two suns ago."

Shock brought Nate to a sitting posture, his right side on fire, to gaze around in bewilderment. There was no sign of the forts. To the left ran a creek, to the right was a hill.

"We have carried you," White Bear revealed. "We do not want you to die yet."

Two days! Nate blinked and pressed his hand to the wound. No wonder the pain wasn't quite as bad as before. And no wonder he was starved.

"You and your friends killed many of my people. You will suffer for each one who died."

Nate looked at his captors again and was pleased to count only nine.

"In another day we will join a war party of our brothers," White Bear disclosed. "Then we shall decide what to do with you."

So he had at least another day of life. Nate glanced at the wound and discovered his shirt had been cut and a gummy substance of some sort applied to the hole. "What is this?"

"An herbal poultice to stop the bleeding and prevent infection," White Bear signed, and saw the incredulity on the youth's countenance.

The illogical practice of patching up a wounded enemy just to kill him later made a perverse sort of sense. Nate knew the Blackfeet delighted in torturing captured enemies, employing the most devious and cruel means imaginable, and since they intended to give him a taste of their savage cruelty, they wouldn't want him to die on them before the event.

A young warrior stepped forward. "I am Red Elk, the one who tended you."

Nate automatically signed, "Thank you." He was surprised when the warrior's mouth creased in an apparently genuine smile.

White Bear scowled and glanced at Red Elk, and perhaps because he had just been using sign language and felt no need to resort to his own tongue, or perhaps because he wanted Nate to know what he said, he addressed Red Elk in the same manner. "Remember he is our enemy and must be slain. All whites are our enemies."

"Even the white who saved my life?"

Some of the others growled in agreement.

"A white saved your life?" Nate inquired.

"Two winters ago," Red Elk related. "I was out hunting by myself far south of our village and tried to cross a frozen river. The ice broke. Try as I might, I could not climb out. I thought the cold would kill me or I would drown. But after a time a lone white trapper came by. He used a rope to pull me out and then made a fire so I could get warm." Red Elk paused. "That trapper saved my life. The next morning he left and I never saw him again."

White Bear snorted. "The only reason he saved you was because he did not know you were a Blackfoot. Had he known he would have left you in the freezing water."

"I do not know that."

"Why else did he save you?" White Bear asked.

Nate saw Red Elk's troubled expression, and realized he really owed his herbal treatment to the unknown trapper who had saved the warrior's life. Red Elk had tended to him out of a sense of obligation to whites in general. Whatever the case, he was glad. And he was surprised to discover not all Blackfeet viewed trappers as implacable foes.

White Bear stood and barked directions. He looked at Red Elk and spoke scornfully for a bit, then moved off to lead the band northward.

"You must get on your feet," Red Elk told Nate.

Using his palms to push erect, Nate swayed and almost pitched onto his face. He righted himself with a supreme effort and took a tentative stride. "I am weak," he informed the Blackfoot. "I do not know if I can keep up."

"If you do not, White Bear will chop off a few of your fingers."

The added incentive sufficed to compel Nate forward. He gained strength with every step. Loud growling in his stomach reminded him of his hunger. "I am starving. When can I eat?"

"When we do," Red Elk answered. He gazed at the backs of his fellow tribesmen, who were all hastening off at a brisk clip. "I am sorry, Grizzly Killer. I would not treat you like this, but I am not the leader of the war party."

"I understand."

"White Bear has placed me in charge of you. If you try to escape, I will be forced to kill you."

"One way or the other I will die," Nate said.

"Yes."

They hiked in silence for half an hour, Nate doing his best to keep up. The Blackfoot apparently weren't concerned about him fleeing; they hardly paid any attention to him except to glance over their shoulders every so often and sneer. He desperately craved food and drink and longed to stop, but he took the threat of losing his fingers seriously and plodded onward, a dull ache in his side, his stomach berating him in a marvelous imitation of an enraged grizzly.

"Are you well enough to converse?" Red Elk inquired as they trudged over the crest of a ridge.

"Yes," Nate replied, eager to do anything to take

his mind off his suffering.

"I imagine you know that most of my people hate whites."

"I got that impression."

"Do you know why?"

"I was told it is because when the first party of whites to ever visit your territory passed through, they killed a Blackfoot," Nate answered, referring to the incident involving the famed Lewis and Clark expedition.

Lewis had separated from his companion to explore land in the vicinity of Maria's River, taking six men along, and his party ran into a small band of Blackfeet. A fight broke out when the Indians attempted to steal some guns. One Blackfoot was stabbed to death, another shot in the stomach, and the rest fled. Ever since the Blackfeet had killed whites indiscriminately.

"They were not the first party," Red Elk said. "Other whites had visited our people and we always treated them with kindness and fairness." He frowned. "Those warriors who tried to steal guns shamed our tribe."

Nate glanced at him. "Do other Blackfeet feel the same way you do?"

"Yes."

"Then why do your people go out of their way to kill my people?"

"The white-haters are the ones who kill so many trappers. The rest of us will not attack whites unless we are attacked first."

"It is sad your leaders do not feel as you do."

"Some of our leaders do. Some do not."

"White Bear is obviously one who does."

"No one hates whites more than he does. It took me much talk to persuade him to let me put a poultice on your wounds, and I was surprised when e finally agreed."

"He wants me alive for whatever torture he has
planned," Nate signed.

"I am afraid you are right." Red Elk looked into
Nate's eyes. "I pity you, Grizzly Killer. The last
trapper White Bear captured died a horrible death.
He was staked out on a grizzly trail and eaten alive
by the next bear that came by."

Nate envisioned such a fate and involuntarily
shuddered.

"There is one good thing," Red Elk said.

"What is that?"

"White Bear never kills an enemy the same way
twice. He will come up with a new means of killing
you."

They lapsed into silence, and for several more
hours Nate endured constant torment. He gritted his
teeth to keep from crying out and showing any
weakness. When White Bear finally called a halt near
a spring, Nate sank to the ground in relief. Another
warrior brought over three strips of dried deer meat,
which Nate consumed in less than a minute. He ate
so fast, he felt sick. A drink of cold mountain water
settled his stomach and revived him considerably.
Still, he moved with difficulty when White Bear
instructed the band to resume their trek.

The rest of the day was more of the same. When
the sun sank to the west they stopped on the south
bank of a narrow stream. Red Elk and a second
warrior stood guard while the rest constructed two
forts. Hunters were sent out to secure meat. Another
caught a few fish.

Nate was prodded at lance point into one of the
forts, and he sat there alone until Red Elk carried
a makeshift bark plate containing roasted deer meat
and fish. Nate ate hungrily even though the food
practically burned his tongue.

Red Elk stayed and watched him eat. When th
final morsel was consumed, he gestured at th
doorway. "You can drink from the stream if yo
wish. I would advise you to do so. You will get n
more food or drink until morning."

"There is something else I must also do."

"What?"

"You know."

Red Elk's forehead creased in perplexity. "I hav
no idea what you are talking about."

"I need to relieve myself."

This elicited a laugh from the young Blackfoo
"You can go, but I am required to watch you th
whole time."

"If you must, you must," Nate said. It would b
pointless to argue. He had to make the best of th
situation until an opportunity to escape presente
itself. If one did. So he let the Blackfoot escort hin
to the spring and drank until he couldn't drin
another sip, then walked behind a tree and did hi
private business.

Red Elk discreetly stayed a few yards away an
pretended to be fascinated by a nearby boulder.

Once Nate was back in the fort, Red Elk sat nea
the doorway. He seemed preoccupied and signe
nothing.

Nate was appalled when two warriors came in an
bound his wrists and ankles, just like the Blackfee
had done with Shakespeare and Baxter. One of then
shoved him onto his left side, then both laughed a
they departed. Now he was deprived of his sol
means of communication.

Not until twilight draped the landscape did severa
Blackfeet enter and build a fire, making themselve
as comfortable as they could.

What a night! Nate had to endure the agony of hi
wound and the taunts and barbs of the trio, who

constantly mocked him and poked him with a lance. Red Elk did not participate. All four Blackfeet eventually fell asleep, and snored loud enough to rouse a hibernating black bear.

Nate attempted to sleep, but couldn't at first. He tried to free his hands and failed.

Wolves howled not far off, yet not one Indian stirred.

An owl hooted close by.

Nate listened to the sounds, his soul dominated by despair, and tried to refrain from thinking about the fate in store for him. Think about Shakespeare, he told himself. Think about his best friend in all creation being safe and sound. Think about his parents and family back in New York, who would, thankfully, be spared the knowledge of his grisly demise. And think about Winona, his darling Winona, who would mourn him and sing an ancient Shoshone chant in honor of his passing.

What a terrible way to end a life!

He wanted to rant and rave, to have a tantrum of epic proportions to protest his unjust fortune. Was this his just reward for a life lived decently, for always doing unto others as he would have them do unto him? Granted, he hadn't attended church as regularly as he should, but he'd never taken the Lord's name in vain, never killed wantonly or abused a woman or child. So why should he end his earthly days in the clutches of a murderous savage? It wasn't *fair*!

Nate twisted his head to stare at the smoke drifting out the opening at the top of the fort. A few stars were visible. He longed to be on his mare, riding at a gallop across a verdant plain, the breeze on his face and joy in his heart. He didn't want to die, not when he had his whole life ahead of him. Somehow, some way, he *must* get loose.

His eyelids drooped and his left cheek sagged to the ground. An earthy scent filled his nostrils. Earth. The natural cloak for a corpse. Would the Blackfeet bury him or leave his body for the scavengers? What a stupid question. They would leave his remains for the buzzards to peck at and the maggots to gorge on. With this ghastly image in his troubled mind, he drifted into a fitful sleep.

Chapter Fifteen

Nate awoke to the sensation of someone poking him in the ribs, and opened his eyes to stare up in befuddled confusion at a smirking Blackfoot warrior. For a few seconds he forgot where he was and what had happened, until his harrowing ordeal came back in a rush and prompted him to sit up and glare at his tormentor.

The warrior laughed and exited the fort.

With a start, Nate realized he was alone. His wound ached dully and his buckskins felt clammy. He lifted his arms and inspected the cord binding his wrists, thinking he would tear into it with his teeth. Before he could, in came Red Elk.

"Hello, Grizzly Killer. I will untie you," the young Blackfoot said, and quickly did as he promised. "Does that feel better?"

"Yes," Nate signed awkwardly, his hands and feet tingling. He flexed his fingers and rotated his ankles in an attempt to restore his constricted circulation.

"We are leaving soon. Would you like dried buffalo meat for breakfast?"

"I would be grateful."

Red Elk nodded and departed to fetch the food.

Another day in the hands of the Blackfeet! Nate frowned at the prospect. Perhaps, though, an opportunity might arise for him to flee. If so, the Blackfeet wouldn't find him as easy to recapture as Baxter. He was fleet of foot and knew it; few of his childhood companions had ever matched his speed and he'd won practically every race he ever entered. He'd always liked to run, and had often done it for exercise. If the chance came up he'd be off like a shot.

A minute later Red Elk entered and gave him a half-dozen pieces of meat.

"Thank you," Nate signed. He bit off a mouthful and chewed heartily.

"Today we will join up with another war party," Red Elk mentioned. "The man who leads it is Chief Medicine Bottle. He is a wise and decent warrior, and I will ask him in private to spare your life."

Nate stopped chewing. "Do you really think he will?"

"I do not know. Even if Medicine Bottle should want to let you go, White Bear will oppose the idea and he has much influence in our councils."

Against his better judgment Nate let his hopes climb. "Who will make the final decision?"

"They might let the warriors take a vote."

"Then I am doomed."

Red Elk's lips compressed. "Do not give up hope as long as there is breath in your body. The Great Mystery works in mysterious ways, a man never knows from one minute to the next what his destiny will be."

"You have great wisdom for one so young," Nate said as a compliment.

"My father, Curly Hair, was known far and wide as a man of outstanding intelligence and his voice always carried exceptional weight in our councils. He taught me well before he was ambushed and killed by lowly Crows."

"I am sorry to hear that."

"Do not be. My father has passed on to a better world where there is always plenty of game and no white men," Red Elk signed, and grinned.

Suddenly a gruff voice bellowed outside.

"White Bears wants you," Red Elk translated.

Clutching the dried meat in his left hand, Nate went out the doorway on his hands and knees and rose. The cool air refreshed him. To the east a rosy glow emanated from below the eastern horizon.

White Bear and the other warriors were conversing. They all fell silent and the tall Blackfoot turned to Nate.

"We must make haste today if we are to reach the rendezvous point with our brothers. You will keep up or I will slice off your ears. Do you understand?"

"Yes," Nate responded, gesturing defiantly.

A wicked sneer curled the hateful warrior's countenance. "I hope you cannot keep up, white dung. Your ears would look nice on the wall of my lodge."

Nate clenched his fists, his blood boiling, but maintained his self-control.

"We go," White Bear stated, and then spoke loudly in his own tongue. Off he strode, taking the lead, and the rest dutifully followed.

The morning hours went by quickly. Nate felt better the farther he walked. Apparently he had not lost enough blood to pose a threat to his life and his organs were all intact. The buffalo meat barely filled his stomach, but they stopped once to drink at a stream and simply quenching his thirst did wonders for his constitution. Several times he tried to draw Red Elk into sign conversation. The warrior was polite but unresponsive and Nate gave up the attempt.

White Bear led them along valleys, over hills, and around jagged peaks. By noon they were descending a slope into a wide valley distinguished by a lake in the center.

"We will meet Medicine Bottle there," Red Elk signed, and nodded at the simmering body of water.

Anxiety surged anew in Nate. Soon his fate would be decided. All morning he had waited for the perfect opportunity to run, but although he was at the rear of the line, there were always Blackfeet gazing over their shoulders and watching him. Then too, he didn't know how much trust he could safely bestow on Red Elk. If he ran, would the warrior be compelled to plant an arrow between his shoulder blades? Obligations were one thing and tribal loyalties quite another, and he was unsure which would win out in the warrior's heart if he put them to the test.

They were still half a mile from the lake when figures were spotted moving about and smoke from several fires began rising skyward. White Bear called a halt. Although he believed it was Medicine Bottle's party, he decided to be on the safe side and sent a warrior ahead to check. Soon the man returned with news that Medicine Bottle was indeed there, having just arrived, and a freshly killed buck was being butchered for a feast.

All these facts Red Elk relayed for Nate's benefit. Nate chided himself for being an idiot and not trying to escape anyway, because now it was too late. He counted 20 warriors near the lake. The odds against him had increased drastically.

White Bear hailed those setting up the camp, and soon the two war parties were mingling and talking excitedly, recounting their exploits since they'd separated to raid the Utes.

Nate saw a short, stocky, elderly Indian in earnest discussion with White Bear.

"That is Chief Medicine Bottle," Red Elk revealed.

Many were the narrowed eyes cast in Nate's direction. He read loathing and enmity in many faces. But in one visage there was only curiosity tinged with a trace of sadness. Chief Medicine Bottle stared at him for a full minute. Nate smiled in return and moved his hands to say, "I have heard you are a fair man. I am happy to meet you."

The chief displayed no reaction and did not answer, but his discussion with White Bear became more animated.

"The other war party did not locate a Ute village either," Red Elk disclosed. "They found a spot where many lodges had been camped, but the Utes had gone. If not for your capture, this raid would shame us all."

"What else are they saying?"

"Some of them are very mad we lost six warriors. One man over there wants to cut off your head. Another says your privates should be hacked off and forced down your throat—"

"That is enough," Nate signed, interrupting. "As I said before, I am doomed."

Red Elk motioned at a nearby fire. "Why not rest until the matter is decided."

Gladly Nate complied. Sitting close to the flames, his chin on his knees, he focused on the tips of his moccasins and closed his mind to contemplation of his fate. Or tried to. There was no doubt the Blackfeet would elect to torture him. Once he knew for certain, once they came to grab him, he would fight to the death. If he could grab a weapon they would be forced to kill him on the spot instead of carrying out their fiendish designs, and a speedy end was vastly preferable to slow, lingering torment.

Footsteps crunched on the ground behind him.

Twisting, Nate discovered Chief Medicine Bottle. The older man's eyes seemed to probe into the depths of his being.

"I am told you are known as Grizzly Killer."

"Yes. The name was given to me by a Cheyenne."

"And have you killed many grizzlies?" Medicine Bottle signed.

"Only three."

"That is more than most men, Indian or white. You must be brave, and you will shortly need all of your bravery. In a while a meeting will be called and we will decide what to do with you. A few want to take you to our village. Many others are incensed at the deaths of their brothers and want to kill you now."

"Where do you stand?"

"I will do as the Great Mystery guides me to do." So signing, the stately warrior turned and started to walk off. Red Elk addressed him and they exchanged words. Medicine Bottle glanced down at Nate and grunted, then left.

"What did the two of you talk about?" Nate inquired.

Red Elk walked to the other side of the campfire and sat down. "I asked him to spare your life as I said I would. He told me he will do his best to help. I must guard you while the council is in progress. Would you like to talk or be alone with your thoughts?"

"Talk," Nate responded gratefully. He watched the rest of the warriors gather 20 feet away, to the west. The feast seemed to be momentarily forgotten.

"You do not show any fear. That is good," Red Elk said.

"Perhaps I do not show it outside, but inside I am very afraid," Nate admitted.

"How is your wound?"

"It is the least of my concerns."

Red Elk laughed. "I like you, Grizzly Killer. It is most unfortunate we have met under these circumstances and that I am a Blackfoot and you are just a white. You have the spirit of an Indian, I think."

"I wish I *was* an Indian right about now. A Blackfoot."

The rejoinder brought more laughter from the warrior. "Are all whites like you?"

"No," Nate confessed. "Not at all. There are many different kinds of whites, good and bad, wise and foolish, kind and savage, just like there are different kinds of Blackfeet."

"Yet you and the only other white I ever met are honorable men. If I had the power I would order the hostilities between our people to cease."

How I wish you did, Nate though morosely. He looked at the council again, and saw the Blackfeet seated in a wide circle with Chief Medicine Bottle and White Bear on the north side next to one another. He also spied the warrior who had his Hawken, pouch, and powder horn, and was strongly tempted to race over and try to rip the gun from the man's grasp.

"Would you like food?" Red Elk asked.

"Thank you, no. I could not eat anything."

"Later then."

Nate absently nodded. If there was a later. To occupy himself with something other than morbid feelings of death, he examined the arrow's exit hole, and was relieved to see no trace of blood or infection. Indian herbal remedies were amazing. They possessed curative properties unknown to white doctors and were remarkably effective. He mentally filed the notion to learn as many as he could if he survived.

White Bear stood and discoursed at length with repeated jabs of his finger at Nate. Many cries of acclamation were interjected by the aroused warriors. Lances were rattled against shields, war clubs and tomahawks waved in the air.

"Do you want to know his words?" Red Elk asked. Why not? "Yes," Nate responded.

"White Bear is telling them you deserve the most horrible death imaginable. Skinning alive is too good for you. He thinks you should be held down while a young rattlesnake is forced down your throat."

"I bet he pulled legs off spiders when he was a child," Nate said.

Chief Medicine Bottle now rose and spoke in slow, measured words, his tone as soothing as a gentle summer's breeze. He also pointed frequently at Nate. Not once did anyone shout. None of the warriors became agitated. They listened attentively and respectfully.

"He is saying you should not be blamed for attacking White Bear's party," Red Elk revealed. "Your friends had been taken and you were only doing as any man would do. He deeply regrets the loss of our brothers, but says killing you will not bring them back or honor their deaths. He believes we should let you go so that you may tell all whites the Blackfeet are an honorable race who do not take base revenge unjustly."

Nate could have hugged the chief. He didn't know the man, and yet here Medicine Bottle was opposing another popular leader to save him. From this day forth he would never again think of the Blackfeet as brutal savages bent only on slaughter. There was dignity to be found in all races of men if one only looked.

After a bit Chief Medicine Bottle took his seat, and then commenced a general debate with most of the warriors voicing their opinions in turn.

"Some agree with Medicine Bottle," Red Elk

explained. "Others side with White Bear."

It was most unfortunate, Nate reflected, that Indian chiefs didn't have the same degree of authority vested in white leaders. While chiefs could try to influence tribal decisions and were considered final arbiters in many matters, they could not dictate policy. Even on raids, individual warriors were permitted to do as they pleased. Indian society enjoyed a level of democracy yet to be attained by the so-called civilized nation existing east of the Mississippi.

The debate went on and on.

Nate saw Red Elk frown at one point and asked, "What is wrong?"

Shaking his head sadly, the warrior responded with, "You will know soon enough."

"Have they decided?"

"No. They are about to vote."

"Then why are you upset?"

"Even honorable people do dishonorable acts when they lose sight of their humanity."

"What?"

"I was quoting my father," Red Elk stated, and would sign no more. He sat with his head bowed, contemplating.

Troubled, Nate glanced at the circle. Chief Medicine Bottle was on his feet again, evidently appealing to each of the warriors one by one to voice their opinion. He went completely around the circle, then closed his eyes.

White Bear did not appear particularly pleased. He frowned and muttered something under his breath when the last of the warriors spoke.

What was happening? Nate wondered, his hopes rising yet again. If White Bear was unhappy, then surely their decision must be good news. Perhaps he would be spared. He saw Medicine Bottle open his eyes and speak, and all the Blackfeet rose and came toward him. Standing, he saw Red Elk coming around the fire and looking very sad. Why?

Chief Medicine Bottle led the Blackfeet, White Bear a stride behind. They halted a yard away and the elderly warrior's kindly eyes regarded Nate with a tinge of regret.

"Grizzly Killer, we have reached a decision," he signed.

"What is it?"

"We have decided you shall not be put to death immediately. Nor will you be tortured."

Nate smiled in partial relief. What did he mean by not put to death *immediately*?

"Instead," Medicine Bottle went on, "you shall run the gauntlet."

Chapter Sixteen

The gauntlet. Two rows of ten warriors, the lines six feet apart, each man armed with a war club, tomahawk, or eyedagg. In this instance the rows extended from north to south, from the shore of the lake into a field. Near the water stood Chief Medicine Bottle, White Bear, and the remaining Blackfeet.

Nate faced the lines and gulped. Every warrior except one grinned at him, eager to smash his skull or rip open his body. He glanced to his right at the chief.

"We are a fair people, Grizzly Killer, despite what you may now believe. You have slain some of our brothers and the warriors of our village demand that you pay a price, but instead of shooting and scalping you on the spot we have voted on a reasonable alternative."

"You call this reasonable?" Nate responded, nodding at the two rows.

"It is more reasonable than tying you to stakes and skinning you alive."

Nate had no argument there.

"You are about to engage in a test of your mettle. Should you prevail, you will be permitted to live. If not, we will take it as an indication you were a cold-hearted murderer and took our brothers' lives out of sheer hatred."

"What must I do?" Nate said, although he knew very well what he must do.

"You will run from this end of the gauntlet to the far end," Medicine Bottle directed. "If you try to break out of the lines you will be shot."

"May I fight back?"

"You may defend yourself as you see fit."

"And once I make it to the far end I am free to go in peace?"

White Bear laughed.

"If you are still alive at the end of the rows you will have completed the first half of your trial," Medicine Bottle patiently answered.

Almost afraid to ask, Nate forced his hands to move and frame the question. "What is the second half?"

"You may run in any direction as fast as you can. Three of our warriors will chase you. If you are caught, they will slay you on the spot. If you elude them you are free."

A snort of contempt came from White Bear. "You will not elude us, white dog. I am one of the three who will give chase, along with Buffalo Horn and Crooked Nose." He indicated two warriors on his right.

Nate looked at their hostile faces and discovered one of his pursuers was to be the warrior who had appropriated the Hawken. "How much of a head start will I be given?"

"None," White Bear signed. "Once you are clear of the lines we will come after you."

Medicine Bottle looked at the tall warrior. "What harm can a slight lead do? Think of the sport he will give you."

Raising his right arm over his eyes to shield them from the bright sun, White Bear scanned the stretch of land past the rows and grinned. "Very well. Do you see the short pine tree, white dog?"

Nate spied a stunted pine approximately one hundred yards distant. "Yes."

"It will be the marker. The moment you pass it, we will give chase."

Of what benefit was a measily one-hundred-yard lead? Nate fumed, and decided to be grateful for the slight advantage Medicine Bottle had manipulated the pugnacious White Bear into giving him. The way things stood, he doubted he would ever reach that tree anyway.

"Now you must take off your clothes," White Bear signed.

"What?" Nate responded in disbelief.

Chief Medicine Bottle nodded. "It is our custom. Any man who runs the gauntlet must do so naked."

"I refuse!" Nate replied angrily.

"Why?" Medicine Bottle queried.

"It is against the customs of my people to go anywhere without clothes on. We consider such behavior a great shame."

White Bear laughed harshly. "Your customs are of no concern to us. You will take off your clothes or we will kill you now." He paused, his lips curled in a mask of wickedness. "Please keep them on."

What should I do? Nate frantically asked himself. Traipsing around naked went against every principle he believed in, every moral precept he'd ever been taught. But if he didn't do as they wanted, he would surely die. If he stripped he would live a while longer. Viewed in such light, he didn't have any choice. "Do I get to keep my moccasins on?" he asked, stalling.

"Nothing," White Bear stated.

All eyes were on Nate as he began removing his garb. He untied his moccasins first and tugged them off, then raised his buckskin shirt. The strain of reaching his arms over his head speared agony through his body but couldn't be helped.

"Hurry, white dog," White Bear declared, using his favorite expression again.

Nate gripped the top of his pants, then paused to glance at the chief. "Must I wait for a signal to begin?"

"You may begin whenever you like," Medicine Bottle revealed.

Good, Nate thought, and bent at the waist as he peeled the buckskin pants from his pale legs, first the right, then the left, deliberately moving slowly, letting them think he was embarrassed or cowed or scared to death or whatever they wanted. Just so they didn't suspect his ulterior motive. They'd expect him to hesitate, to be afraid to enter the gauntlet, and they would be off their guard.

Nate extended his right arm, let the pants fall, and suddenly took off in full stride, his arms and legs flying, staying stooped over to present a smaller target, his eyes darting right and left. The ruse worked. He was past the first two men on each side before the rest awoke to the deception with bellows of rage. From behind him came White Bear's roar. He ignored the noise and concentrated on the warriors. If his attention lapsed for a heartbeat he was dead.

A lean Blackfoot stood on the right, a war club in the hand that he now raised overhead.

Nate saw the man's shoulder muscles tighten and knew the swing was coming. He dodged to the left, nearer the other row, and the club descended, nicking his arm. Ignoring the pain, he pressed on.

On the left was another warrior, this one wielding a tomahawk and grinning in anticipation.

In two bounds Nate was there, twisting to confront his foe as the tomahawk arced down toward his forehead. He leaped in closer, using his left forearm to block the descending swipe, and planted his right fist on the tip of the warrior's nose, flattening him.

Onward he went, never slowing for an instant because to slow down meant he would never see Winona again, never know the joy of a majestic high-country morning once more or witness the radiant hues coloring the heavens as the sun rose and set.

The next Blackfoot had a war club.

Nate ran directly at the man. Part of the rules, if such there were, seemed to entail that the Blackfeet could not stray into the middle of the gauntlet; they must attack from their appointed spots on the sides. Most runners probably stayed in the center and were easily cut down, but he had no intention of doing the same. The Blackfeet weren't going to get him without a battle they would long recall.

Whooping loudly, the next warrior hefted his club and carefully gauged the distance before swinging. Nate didn't bother trying to deflect the Blackfoot's arm this time. He went for the war club, his hands rising to meet it and grasping the wooden handle just below the pointed stone attached to the top. The tip of the stone came within an inch of his left eye before he checked its momentum. He wrenched on the weapon, striving to disarm his foe, but the warrior held on with all his might and hissed, delaying him when he must not be delayed, so instead of continuing to pull he simply let go.

Taken unawares, the warrior's own strength and stance worked against him and he stumbled backward away from the line.

Keep going! Nate's mind screamed, and he did, cognizant of a pain in his side but suppressing the sensation as he closed on another warrior on the left, a skinny man with a long-handled tomahawk.

The man drew the weapon back, his teeth exposed in an animal snarl.

This time Nate knew he must do something different. That long handle ruled out the direct approach, so he tried a clever ploy, waiting until the warrior started his swing and then diving at the man's legs, diving under the sweeping tomahawk and tackling the skinny Blackfoot. They both went down, Nate winding up on top, and he drove his fists in a furious flurry, pounding the warrior's jaw and stunning him. Lunging, Nate grabbed the tomahawk from the man's limp fingers, rose, and raced toward the end of the rows.

The remaining Blackfeet appeared disconcerted by the unique maneuver.

Nate wasn't going to give them the chance to gather their wits. He swung the tomahawk wildly, screeching like a madman, darting at each man in turn, and in turn the first three ducked aside rather than engage him. The rest held their ground and swung their weapons, but they were hampered by having to stay on the side and the fact most of them carried shorter clubs or tomahawks, which put them at a costly disadvantage. Stone and metal and wood clashed, clanged, and smacked together, and in a swirling rush of motion Nate swept past all but the last pair.

They were braced, these two, the man on the left with an eyedagg, a weapon incorporating a wooden handle and an angled metal spike at the end, while the man on the right held a war club.

The man on the right was Red Elk.

Nate had seen White Bear badger the younger warrior, goading the youth into taking a position in the line. Although he hadn't understood the words, he'd guessed that White Bear had called Red Elk's manhood and loyalty to the tribe into question. Under the probing stares of his fellow warriors, Red Elk had had no choice but to take a spot.

And now here he was, ready to attack.

For an instant their eyes met, and Nate registered commingled hurt and anger befor Red Elk's club descended toward his brow. He blocked the blow with the tomahawk and instantly pivoted to face the other Blackfoot, who surprised him by leaping forward and employing the eyedagg with both hands in an overhand strike.

Nate ducked to the left, evading the spike, and at the moment he shifted he saw Red Elk materialize in the very spot he'd just vacated. He tried to shout a warning, but he could do nothing more than gape in shocked horror as the eyedagg struck Red Elk between the eyes and bored several inches into the warrior's flesh and bone.

Red Elk's eyes widened, his arms went limp, and his entire body quivered violently.

The other Blackfoot, aghast at his mistake, gaped at his tribesman in an appalled daze.

Enraged at Red Elk's senseless death, Nate buried the edge of his tomahawk in the Blackfoot's neck, severing a vein or artery, causing blood to gush out. He yanked the blade out and dashed past the sputtering Blackfoot, into the open, wondering if he would get an arrow or a ball in the back before he covered ten yards. Incredibly, he didn't, and he focused on the stunted pine, running all out.

The reality of his achievement sank in. He'd done it! Survived the gauntlet! But he still had to outrun three fleet Blackfeet when he was already in pain and winded. The naked soles of his feet padded on the grass and weeds. Occasionally he stepped on a sharp stone or twig and flinched. No matter how much it hurt, he determined he wasn't stopping for hell or high water.

Harsh shouts arose to his rear.

Nate was tempted to look back and see if White Bear and the others had violated the agreement, but he didn't want to break his stride. Twenty yards beyond the stunted pine grew a verdant expanse of woodland. If he could reach those trees, he might be able to shake the trio of avenging furies.

He glanced at a snow-crowned peak to the south and succumbed to momentary despair. Even if he should, by some miracle, elude White Bear, Crooked Nose, and Buffalo Horn, how was he going to survive alone and naked in the wilderness, his sole weapon a tomahawk? If he encountered a grizzly the outcome would be a foregone conclusion.

Nate drew nearer to the pine. His left foot came down hard on a sharp stone and he stumbled, almost going down. He reestablished his running rhythm and sped on, feeling moist drops on his left sole. The stone had cut him. He hoped the laceration wasn't serious because he couldn't stop to check.

Each second became an eternity as he ran, ran, ran. Nate was still five yards from the stunted pine when tremendous cheers from the vicinity of the lake heralded the unleashing of the undoubtedly eager pursuers. He didn't bother to look until he reached the forest and paused to gulp in air.

The three incensed Blackfeet were bounding in pursuit, White Bear in the lead.

Spinning, Nate dashed into the woods and immediately angled to the east, weaving among the trees, thickets, and boulders. Broken limbs and shattered branches lay in profusion on the ground, any one of which could tear open his feet and legs, and he was kept busy avoiding such normally harmless obstacles.

After traveling 20 yards Nate slanted to the south again, opting for a zigzag course to make tracking him more difficult, hopefully slowing down the warriors. Despite his best efforts he was repeatedly jabbed and speared by the vegetation he passed, crisscrossing his skin with tiny red slash marks.

Nate glanced over his shoulder time and again, but saw no sign of the Blackfeet. As the minutes went by and the trio still didn't appear, he became mystified. Blackfeet warriors, like most Indians, were fast runners. A lifetime spent in the wilderness, of hunting and raiding and living on the raw edge of existence, hardened Indian men and endowed them with extraordinary speed and stamina. He should have seen them by now. Why hadn't he?

Think!

He tried to reason as they would, plan as they would. Since they had seen him race to the woods, White Bear and the other two were aware of his own capability. Perhaps they had reasoned they couldn't hope to overtake him, which seemed a ridiculous notion but was the only explanation he could think of.

What would they do then?

Think!

They must know the lay of the land better than he did since they had selected the lake as a rendezvous point. Was it possible for them to get ahead of him? Was there a shortcut? He grinned at his stupidity. Here he was, fleeing due south along the verdant basin of a valley. There was no way they could take any shortcut that would bring them in front of him.

Still puzzled, Nate raced deeper into the woods, farther from the war party. Every stride he took raised his confidence a notch higher. Once he escaped, he could devote his attention to securing clothing and food.

A twig snapped off to the right.

Gazing in that direction, Nate gasped in astonishment at spying one of the Blackfeet 40 feet away, parallel with his position, effortlessly keeping pace. Bewildered, he glanced to the left and saw the warrior who had taken the Hawken an equal distance away. The Blackfeet weren't trying to overtake him; they already had! Now they were playing with him before moving in for the kill!

Chapter Seventeen

Nate instantly increased his pace, his sinews straining, his feet thudding on the ground.

Both Indians did likewise, each grinning wickedly.

Ahead appeared a low knoll.

Nate slowed a bit and saw them do the same. The chilling realization that he was at their mercy aroused a spark of self-recriminatin. What a fool he'd been! White Bear must have selected the fastest runners in the war party, warriors who could easily overtake him, who didn't need to stick to his exact trail. For that matter, they'd undoubtedly surmissed he would be heading back into the heart of Ute country, which meant going south.

Damn his idiocy!

The recrimination changed to indignation. He resolved to fight to the last. Since he couldn't hope to outrun them, he must resort to strategy. But what to do? He gazed at the knoll and an idea blossomed.

Both warriors were still staying abreast of him. Good. If they continued to do so, they would each skirt the knoll, one passing by on the right, the other the left, leaving him to go up and over. For a few seconds as he neared the top he would be out of their sight.

Nate gripped the tomahawk handle tighter and steeled his body. He made the knoll and started up, keeping his eyes fixed straight ahead so he wouldn't give away his intentions. When only three yards from the top he quickly looked to both sides and watched the warriors spring past the sides of the low hillock. Abruptly halting, he wheeled to the left, bent at the waist, and ran toward the bottom, not stopping until he came to a wide tree and crouched in the shelter of the trunk.

He envisioned the two Blackfeet stopping and gazing in confusion at the crest of the knoll when he failed to appear. They would naturally hasten back to investigate his disappearance. If the Great Mystery smiled on him, they would simply retrace their steps. The warrior carrying his rifle would pass within a few feet of his position. The rest would be up to Nate.

He peeked around the trunk and tingled at the sight of the warrior already heading back and staring in perplexity up at the knoll. Since the man's nose bore no evidence of a break, he deduced this one must be Buffalo Horn.

The Blackfoot trotted slowly, the Hawken in his left hand. He wore only buckskin pants and moccasins. On his left hip hung a knife in a beaded sheath.

Keep coming! Nate thought.

Clearly confused, Buffalo Horn raised his right arm and waved.

Nate looked and saw Crooked Nose, an arrow notched to the bow he held, rounding the opposite side of the knoll, similarly searching. Crooked Nose returned the wave and shook his head. Nate glanced at Buffalo Horn.

The Blackfoot was ten feet away, eyes roving over the slope, probing every shadow, every nook and cranny. He rotated slowly to the left, gazing to the south, his back to the tree.

Nate might never have a better chance. He launched himself from concealment and charged, the tomahawk uplifted, and heard Crooked Nose shout a warning.

Buffalo Horn whirled and started to level the rifle, amazement lining his features.

I'm not going to make it! Nate thought. He still had six feet to go and the Hawken was almost even with his stomach, so he did the only thing he could think of; he threw the tomahawk at the Blackfoot's head. Having never thrown a tomahawk before, he expected to do no more than force the warrior to duck and buy himself the seconds he needed to reach the Blackfoot. He certainly never expected to score a hit. But he did.

The tomahawk flew end over end and the razor-sharp blade caught Buffalo Horn full on the nose, splitting both nostrils and eliciting a scream from the terrified man. The tomahawk stuck fast, and Buffalo Horn let go of the rifle and grabbed the handle to yank the weapon out. Blood flowed copiously.

Nate dove, landing on his right shoulder and rolling the final yard to rise to his knees at Buffalo Horn's feet, his fingers closing on the Hawken.

The warrior staggered backward and wrenched the tomahawk free, the suction producing a bubbling sucking sound. His eyes fluttered and his knees buckled. Groaning, he sank down and fell onto his left side.

Nate started to rise as an arrow streaked from his right and missed his head by a hair. He twisted to find Crooked Nose racing toward him.

His face betraying rabid rage, the Blackfoot was notching a second arrow on the bowstring.

Up came the Hawken in a practiced, fluid motion. Nate sighted squarely on the warrior's chest, cocked the hammer, and fired. The booming blast was sweeter to his ears than the most melodious music ever created by mortal man.

The ball took the Blackfoot dead center, the impact lifting him from his feet to crash onto his back. Crooked Nose tried to rise, staring down at the neat, bloody hole in the middle of his chest, then collapsed without a sound.

Silence gripped the forest.

Nate looked from one to the other, thinking they might still rise, that he couldn't possibly have defeated them both. After a minute he stood and walked over to Buffalo Horn, convinced he had triumphed. Two down and one to go.

One to go!

White Bear was out there somewhere.

With a start Nate scanned the woods on all sides but saw nothing. Chiding himself for his negligence, he knelt and stripped his powder horn and ammo pouch from Buffalo Horn. He slung both across his chest and hurriedly reloaded, breathing a sigh of relief when the ball and patch were finally shoved home down the barrel. He replaced the rod and scoured the forest again.

Where was White Bear?

He took a step, and his glance fell on the pants and moccasins the dead man wore. Crooked Nose was slightly smaller, but the clothes might fit. He crouched and removed them, then slid into the pants. They were tight but serviceable. In moments the moccasins covered his sore, bleeding, blistering feet. The knife and tomahawk were around his waist. He headed south.

Nervously fingering the trigger, Nate constantly scoured the vegetation for some sign of his enemy. Why hadn't White Bear been with the others? Or had White Bear been out there somewhere and witnessed the whole incident? If so, why hadn't the Blackfoot tried to aid his fellows? The many questions were an annoying distraction, so he shook his head to clear his mind and devoted his full attention to simply staying alive.

Nate covered a quarter of a mile without seeing White Bear. He entertained the idea that the warrior had taken a different course from the others and must be far away.

A mile later he climbed to the top of a rise and stared down at the valley. He could see the lake and smoke curling up from the campfires, but there were no Blackfeet on his heels. Allowing himself the luxury of a victory smile, Nate turned and continued over the rise into the next valley. He had to descend a boulder-strewn slope, moving among giant rocks ten and 12 feet in height. The warm air felt nice on his skin. He touched the arrow wound and found it to be sore.

Halfway down the slope he was compelled to pass between two huge boulders with barely enough space between them for him to squeeze through. He lowered the rifle to his side and eased into the notch, the rough stone scraping his back and chest, then stepped into the clear.

Nate hefted the Hawken and took a pace. A scraping noise to his right made him start to rotate, but a heavy object smashed into the back of his head before he could complete the move. Brilliant points of lights danced in front of his face, dazzling him, and his legs went weak. He tottered and dropped to his right knee, pressing the rifle on the ground for support.

A gleaming streak of light seemed to come out of

nowhere and something struck the rifle barrel a
jarring blow, severely stinging his hand and knocking
the gun loose. He blinked frantically, trying to regain
control, and stiffened when the hard point of a
slender weapon touched his neck.

A few gruff words were spoken mockingly.

Nate recognized the cold voice and tensed. His
vision cleared. He flicked his eyes to the left and
looked up at the malevolent face of White Bear.

The Blackfoot addressed him scornfully, then
stepped back, withdrawing the tip of his sword. He
motioned for Nate to stand.

Slowly, his arms at his sides, Nate rose and glared
at the warrior. He'd been outfoxed, plain and simple,
by that smirking bastard. An urge to clamp his hands
around the Blackfoot's throat seized him, and it was
all he could do to stay still as White Bear wagged the
sword and laughed.

Again the warrior motioned, this time indicating
Nate should walk lower down the slope.

Reluctantly Nate complied, halting when the
Blackfoot barked a word in the tribal tongue, then
turned.

White Bear had not budged. He was 12 feet away,
grinning, and he now did a most surprising thing; he
slid his sword under the cord around his waist.

Nate waited, suspecting a trick.

"At last it is just the two of us, white dog, man to
man," the Blackfoot signed.

Nate didn't bother to respond.

"You are more resourceful than I gave you credit
for being," White Bear went on. "Only two men out
of ten survive the gauntlet."

The Hawken was lying near the Blackfoot's feet.
Nate glanced at it, wishing it was closer.

"Your friend Red Elk did not survive," White Bear
taunted him. "He received the fate he deserved."

The slur against the young warrior prompted Nate to reply. "Why did he deserve to die? Because he felt whites and Blackfeet can live together in peace?"

"Yes. He was a fool."

"He was an honorable man, which is more than I can say for you."

White Bear placed his right hand on the sword's hilt. "I have enjoyed slaying few men as much as I will enjoy slaying you."

"My people have a saying," Nate related, and was about to go into detail about unborn chickens when he realized the warrior had probably never seen one. He adjusted the axiom accordingly. "Never count your birds before they are hatched."

"What birds?"

"Ravens. Jays. Sparrows. Any kind you want."

White Bear nodded. "As I suspected. All whites are crazy." He drew the sword. "Soon there will be one less crazy white in the mountains, one less white to destroy the beaver and kill all the buffalo."

Nate drew the tomahawk.

"I could have killed you at any time, dog," White Bear signed, and pointed at his bow and quiver lying beside a boulder eight feet away. "But that would have been the easy way, the way of a coward. No, I want to kill you in man-to-man combat. I want to see the fear in your eyes and feel my sword cut through your body. When you are dead I will chop your body into pieces for the vultures and the coyotes. All except your hair. Your scalp will hang on my lodge for all my brothers to see."

"First you must take it," Nate countered, "and it will take more than words to do that."

Raising the sword, White Bear sprang to the attack.

Nate barely got the tomahawk up in time to deflect a vicious swipe that would have split his skull like an overripe melon. He quickly backpedaled, blocking blow after blow, the sword biting into the tomahawk's wooden handle again and again, sending chips flying.

White Bear vented a roar of rage and redoubled his efforts.

Dodging to the right, Nate swung at the Blackfoot's legs, only to have the swing expertly countered. The sword point arced at his throat, and he skipped rearward to avoid being impaled. More strikes rained down on him and he staved off each one, but his right arm was rapidly tiring. After all he had been through his body couldn't sustain such a brutal pace indefinitely. He needed to win soon or he would tire and fall easy prey to the gloating warrior.

The Blackfoot sneered as he fought, his face conveying unmitigated contempt, and wielded the sword with remarkable agility. His glittering sword was constantly in motion, slashing and stabbing, a blur of golden light.

Nate was forced to retreat down the slope. He worried about tripping over an unseen obstacle and exposing himself to his enemy. Once he almost did go down when his left heel bumped into a rock and he lost his balance and nearly fell.

White Bear took instant advantage, lancing the point at Nate's throat.

Only by jerking his head to the right did Nate evade the tip. He batted the blade aside with the tomahawk and righted himself, his mind racing, seeking to somehow achieve victory before another such inadvertent blunder cost him his life.

The warrior seemed angered by the miss. He swung with berserk abandon.

Under the savage onslaught Nate felt his arm tiring even faster. Fingernail-sized bits of wood had been hacked from the tomahawk's handle. All other factors being equal, a tomahawk was simply no match for a sword; it was shorter and possessed a smaller cutting edge. The best he could hope to do was block all the Blackfoot's blows.

White Bear evidently realized the tomahawk was all that stood between him and triumph. He concentrated on the handle, repeatedly slicing into the wood in an attempt to chip the tomahawk in half.

Nate knew it was only a matter of time before the Blackfoot would succeed. Once the tomahawk was rendered useless, what did he have left to fight with? The knife?

The knife!

The new surge of vigor coursed through Nate's veins as inspiration provided him with a means of prevailing over his adversary. The hunting knife still hung in its beaded sheath on his left hip. Ever so slowly, his left hand moving at a snail's pace, he inched toward the hilt. He suddenly turned sideways and swung the tomahawk furiously. If he could keep the Blackfoot's attention exclusively on the light axe, his plan would succeed.

Displaying surprise at the unexpected, renewed resistance, White Bear backed up a yard, then held his ground. For the first time since their fight began he was on the defensive.

Nate maintained the pressure, his right arm lashing while his left crept to the knife. His hand wrapped around the hilt. Now all he had to do was find an opening.

White Bear parried yet another blow and speared the sword at the youth's abdomen.

Sliding to the left, Nate stumbled when his foot encountered a shallow depression. He fell onto his left knee, the tomahawk upraised to deflect the sword.

The warrior delivered a terrific blow backed by all

the power in his body, and the keen edge bit clear through the wooden handle and swept downward.

There was no time to react. Nate felt the Spanish sword bite into his right shoulder and threw himself to the rear, landing on his back. A moist sensation indicated the Blackfoot had drawn blood. Nate placed his right palm on the grass and tried to shove erect, but already the tall Blackfoot towered above him with the sword held high for the killing stroke.

White Bear grinned and swung.

Chapter Eighteen

In desperation Nate twisted to the left and the sword struck the ground, missing his ear by a hair. For a moment White Bear's face was close to his and he stared into the warrior's hate-filled eyes. Then he whipped the hunting knife out and around, driving the blade up and into the Blackfoot's chest, all the way in, and twisting.

White Bear's mouth slackened and he uttered a gurgling wheeze. He blinked rapidly and grimaced, then tore himself loose and staggered a few feet, the sword dangling from his right hand.

Nate surged erect and crouched, ready to resist another attack, blood dripping from his knife.

The Blackfoot tried to lift the sword again, but his arm refused to cooperate. He looked down at the blood pumping from the hole in his chest and groaned. His eyes closed for a second and he swallowed hard, then he glanced around and shuffled unsteadily to the right until he collided with a waist-high boulder. The sword fell. He sank to the ground with his back to the boulder and looked at Nate. "You have won, white dog," he signed sluggishly.

Nate lowered the knife.

"I am bleeding badly inside. I can feel it," White Bear said.

Squatting, Nate wiped the hunting knife clean on a small bush.

"Finish me off."

Nate replaced the knife in its sheath and straightened.

"Finish me off."

"Why should I?" Nate asked, walking over to pick up the sword.

"I am too weak to fight, to even stand. All I can do is sit here and bleed to death. This is no way for a warrior to die. Kill me so I can go to the next world with dignity."

"No."

White Bear attempted to lift his arms. Suddenly he coughed and blood trickled from the left corner of his mouth. "See? This is a horrible way to die. Kill me, now, or I will curse you. I will call on the spirits of the air and the land to destroy you."

Nate started to turn.

The warrior scowled and lightly smacked the earth at his side. "White dog! I knew you had no honor the first time I laid eyes on you. All whites are the same. None of you know anything about the ways of the Great Mystery, about the proper ways to live and die. You do not treat your enemies with respect because you do not know how to respect yourselves. You are cowards, all of you. You do not deserve to be called men!" Further weakened by moving his arms and hands, White Bear sagged, a crimson streak now issuing from the right side of his mouth also.

Pivoting, Nate studied the warrior's countenance, studied the almost palpable animosity, and came to a decision.

White Bear grinned and raised his hands one last time. "Do you have any honor, white dog? If so, prove it."

Nate did.

The sun hung an hour above the western horizon when he emerged from a stretch of forest and began hiking across a wide meadow. His entire body ached, and many lacerations stung terribly, and both the arrow and sword wounds hurt intensely. He suppressed the pain and marched onward.

A pair of elk were grazing to the east. They calmly watched him approach, their gums rising and falling as they chewed.

Nate gazed at them, debating whether to shoot one for his supper, then glanced to the south and halted.

A large body of riders was heading directly toward him. They were Indians.

Since they would be on him before he could hope to reach the shelter of the trees, and suspecting they would turn out to be hostile, he raised the Hawken and took a bead on one of those in the lead, realizing as he did that two of those riders were white men. He lowered the rifle and waited.

One of the white men waved.

Amazement washed over Nate as he recognized Shakespeare and Baxter. Sweet relief flooded his soul and he returned the wave.

The mountain man was astride his white horse and leading Nate's mare. Baxter had their other animals on a string.

Not until the riders were 30 yards off did Nate recognize the warrior riding on Baxter's right as Two Owls. He placed the stock of his rifle on the grass and leaned on the barrel, grinning happily.

There were over 50 Indians in all, and they formed into a semicircle around him as they drew to a halt.

"Nate!" Shakespeare bellowed, and vaulted from

his mount to dash up and embrace the younger man. He stopped with his arms outstretched, gazing at the wounds, cuts, and bruises, and snorted. "Lord, son, you're a mess. Have you been playing in the briar patch again?"

Chuckling, Nate gave his mentor a hug, then stepped back and asked in a suddenly raspy voice, "Are you all right? I was worried sick about you."

"Never felt better." Shakespeare looked to the north. "Where are the Blackfeet? We saw them take you, but there wasn't a thing we could do about it."

"The war party met up with another one at a lake north of here. They might still be there."

"They just upped and let you go, did they?"

"I escaped," Nate said, and left it at that. He glanced at Two Owls and signed, "It is good to see you again."

"I am glad you still live, Grizzly Killer," the Ute replied. He gestured proudly at the other warriors. "My people came to help us after the village was safely moved."

"Did you know Two Owls is their chief?" Shakespeare mentioned.

Nate's surprise showed. "Why did you keep it a secret?" he asked the Ute.

"What difference does it make? Chiefs are only ordinary men. When they start thinking they are special they deserve to be smeared with buffalo manure and made to eat grass." Two Owls stared northward. "We are going to punish the Blackfeet for trying to raid our village. Would you like to come?"

"Another time," Nate answered. He walked to the mare, stroked her neck, and swung into the saddle.

"I guess now we can tend to our beaver trapping," Shakespeare said. "We recovered all the traps so we can start whenever you want."

"Next month, maybe."

"What?"

"You wanted some time to yourself, as I recall. Well, you can have it. If you're of a mind, swing by my cabin in a month and you can teach me more about trapping then."

"You're going home?"

"As fast as I can." Nate glanced at Baxter. "Would you be so kind as to remove my two pack animals from the string."

"Sure. Glad to." The Ohioan climbed down to do as he was requested.

"What happened to you?" Shakespeare inquired.

"Nothing."

"Then why are you in such an all-fired hurry to get home?"

Nate touched the hole in his side. "The best woman in the world is back there anxiously waiting for me to return. I don't want to keep her waiting."

"What harm would another few weeks do?"

Nate looked at the mountain man. "Didn't you once tell me that a long time ago you were deeply in love with a Flathead woman?"

"Yes," Shakespeare said softly.

"And I know you have almost met your Maker a time or two."

"I have," Shakespeare conceded.

"Then you should be able to understand," Nate said, and moved over to take the leads to his pack animals from Baxter. "Thank you."

"Sorry to see you go. Take care of yourself."

"You too. Don't keep your family waiting," Nate said, and turned to the Ute chief. "May the Great Mystery guide your every footstep."

"And yours, Grizzly Killer."

Finally Nate stared at the mountain man, his eyes conveying the depth of his affection. "Do you understand now?"

"I believe I do."

"No hard feelings?"

"You know better."

Smiling gratefully, Nate faced eastward and galloped off.

For a minute no one spoke or signed a word.

Baxter broke the silence. "Now what was all that about?" he wondered aloud.

The frontiersman sighed. "Would you like some advice, Thaddeus?" he asked while watching the youth recede in the distance.

"I'm always open to reasonable suggestions."

"Good. Then do that wife of yours a favor and either go back to Ohio or divorce her."

"I don't believe in divorce."

Shakespeare glanced at him and beamed. "Then you shouldn't have any trouble making up your mind."

Epilogue

She was seated on a log near the cabin, her head bowed, her long, raven hair hanging down past her knees. A sleeveless leather dress clung to her slender figure and moccasins adorned her small feet. Leaning down, she used a finger to draw the likeness of a cradleboard in the dirt, humming as she etched the lines.

Intuition made her stiffen and stand. She sensed the presence of someone else and spun in alarm, her incipient fear changing to dominating joy when she spied the man on horseback and the pair of pack animals he led. Her eyes brightened and she ran to meet him, voicing one of the few English words she knew. "Nate! Nate!"

He galloped the rest of the way and jumped from the mare before the animal had stopped. In a rush he swept her into his arms and held her tight, savoring the feel of her and the scent of her hair and never wanting to let her go. "Winona," he said, nearly choking on the word.

After a time she pushed back and stared in shock at his battered body. "What happened?" she signed. "Where is Shakespeare?"

"We ran into some Blackfeet," Nate revealed, and quickly added, "Shakespeare is fine. He will stop to see us during the next moon."

"Where is your shirt?" Winona asked, and looked at his legs. "And where are the pants you wore when you left?"

"It is a long story and I will tell you the details later," Nate pledged. He tenderly kissed her. "I have ridden hard to get here, and now all I want to do is lie in bed with you for a week."

Winona grinned. "What do you have in mind?"

"We can try to make that baby you have been talking about?"

"There is no need."

"Why?" Nate asked.

As she placed her hands on her abdomen, Winona's grin widened. Then she signed, "Because we have already made our baby."

"We have?" Nate responded, and her meaning sank home. "We have!" he repeated, joyously, impulsively taking her in his arms and whirling her about. Suddenly he stopped and set her down. "Sorry. I should not be so rough," he signed.

"I will not break."

"So you say. But until the baby is born I will handle all the difficult chores. You just take it easy."

Winona giggled. "Perhaps I should be with child more often."

Nate embraced her, and for that sweet moment in time and eternity they shared a supreme bliss and their souls soared on the uplifting currents of mutual abiding love.

DOUBLE-BARREL WESTERNS

Twice the Action —
Twice the Adventure —
Only a Fraction of the Price!

Two complete and unabridged novels in each book!

NOTCHED GUNS and **TROUBLE RIDES TALL**
by William Hopson
__2944-8 $3.95

CHEYENNE LANCE and **MEDICINE WAGON**
by John Legg
__2994-4 $3.95

DOUBLE PONY SOLDIERS: SLAUGHTER AT BUFFALO CREEK / COMMANCE MASSACRE
by Chet Cunningham
__3003-9 $3.95

DOUBLE PREACHER'S LAW: WIDOW MAKER / TRAIL OF DEATH
by Dean McElwain
__3002-0 $3.95

DOUBLE-BARREL WESTERNS
Twice the Action —
Twice the Adventure —
Only a Fraction of the Price!

Two complete and unabridged novels in each book!

Hell to Hallelujah and **Ride to the Gun**
by Ray Hogan.

__2917-0 $3.95

Hangman's Range and **Saddle Pals**
by Lee Floren.

__2913-8 $3.95

Vengeance Valley and **Wildhorse Range**
by Allan K. Echols.

__2928-6 $3.95

LEISURE BOOKS
ATTN: Customer Service Dept.
276 5th Avenue, New York, NY 10001
Please add $1.25 for shipping and handling of the first book and $.30 for each book thereafter. All orders shipped within 6 weeks via postal service book rate.

Canadian orders must reflect Canadian price, when indicated, and must be paid in U.S. dollars through a U.S. banking facility.

Name _____

Address _____

City _____ State _____ Zip _____

I have enclosed $ _____ in payment for the books checked above.

Payment <u>must</u> accompany all orders.   ❑Please send a free catalogue.